W9-BBA-616

Norma Farber

MERCY SHORT

A Winter Journal, North Boston, 1692–93

A UNICORN BOOK   E. P. DUTTON   NEW YORK

Special thanks are due the Boston Atheneum
for the loan of books concerned with the time
and place of this book.

Copyright © 1982 by Norma Farber

All rights reserved. No part of this publication may be
reproduced or transmitted in any form or by any means,
electronic or mechanical, including photocopy, recording,
or any information storage and retrieval system now
known or to be invented, without permission in writing
from the publisher, except by a reviewer who wishes to
quote brief passages in connection with a review written
for inclusion in a magazine, newspaper, or broadcast.

Library of Congress Cataloging in Publication Data

Farber, Norma.
Mercy Short: a winter journal, North Boston, 1692–93.
"A Unicorn book."

Summary: With the help of the respected minister
Cotton Mather, a young girl attempts to recover from her
tragic experience with the Indians which has led her
to believe she is bewitched.
[1. New England—Social life and customs—Colonial period,
ca. 1600–1775—Fiction.   2. Witchcraft—Fiction.
3. Mather, Cotton, 1663–1728—Fiction]   I. Title.
PZ7.F2228Me   1982   [Fic]   82-5013
ISBN 0-525-44014-3   AACR2

Published in the United States by E. P. Dutton, Inc.,
2 Park Avenue, New York, N.Y. 10016

Published simultaneously in Canada by Clarke,
Irwin & Company Limited, Toronto and Vancouver

Editor: Emilie McLeod   Designer: Riki Levinson

Printed in the U.S.A.   First Edition
10 9 8 7 6 5 4 3 2

WEN
PZ
7
.F2228
Me
1982

FRANKLIN PIERCE COLLEGE
LIBR
RINDG.. N.. HAMPS; RE

for Emilie, who asked for a novel

Mercy Short had been taken captive by our cruel and bloody Indians in the East, who at the same time horribly butchered her father, her mother, her brother, her sister, and others of her kindred and then carried her and three surviving brothers with two sisters from Salmon Falls, New Hampshire unto Canada: after which our fleet returning from Quebec to Boston, brought them with other prisoners that were then redeemed.

We were informed partly from the speeches that fell from her in her trances; partly from the accounts by her afterwards given unto me.
       —Cotton Mather,
          BRAND PLUCK'D OUT OF THE BURNING,
          BEING AN ACCOUNT OF MERCY SHORT, WHO
          WAS SUPPOSED TO SUFFER BY WITCHCRAFT

1692

Dec. 5

Mr. Mather has asked me to put it down on paper. He has given me this bundle of blank sheets from his desk. As often as the cursed Specters forget to torment me, whenever I can so much as hold quill in hand without its being wrenched and hurled away by their Witchcraft, I am to record what they have done to me. Thus, Mr. Mather will have an account of their Devilry and will be the better able to deal with it. He is a Godly man, and though considerably younger than my father, Clement Short, would be— had the Savages but spared him—Mr. Mather is like a loving father to me. Repeatedly I ask Mr. Mather to speak the comforting words from CORINTHIANS: *And I . . . will be a father to you.* He proposes we sing a psalm together. I choose the one I loved best back in Salmon Falls—can it be nearly three years ago?— *Though my thoughts from Thee may stray.* The third verse is so beautiful.

> *Yet Thy heart to me below*
> *Is inclined in love, I know,*
> *As a father's faithfully,*
> *And will never turn from me.*

Yes, he shall be as a father to me. Or a beloved elder brother, or cousin. A cousin, Mr. Mather being not yet thirty years of age. I, Mercy Short, am barely seventeen. In the moments when I am free of the Furies, I feel confident he will rescue me from torture and harassment.

Yesterday, the Lord's Day, sitting at the meetinghouse beside my mistress, I was at first greatly comforted by Mr. Mather's sermon. His voice is like a noble angel speaking, slowly, deliberately. It drowns out the baleful screeches of Redman talk that persist in haunting me. I can almost forget that vicious Tawny Indian who struck down my mother to her death, and later, on the march, my sister Deliverance and brother Ebenezer. Poor girl, what kind of Deliverance awaited her? And Eben, whose name signifies Stone of Help, where was his Help in need? The rest of us, including three brothers and two sisters who had been spared with me, plodded on toward Quebec in the certainty that we were being held for eventual massacre. It is a miracle the Boston fleet, under Sir William Phips, arrived in time, some eight months later, to redeem us—all except my brother Richard. I suspect the French have by now converted him into a Fiendish Catholic.

I must have been carried to this dwelling directly from the meetinghouse, along Bell Alley, and placed under this fine roof, my mistress's house being too far away. The wealthy merchant and his wife who have kindly taken me in are among those who contributed to the price of my ransom. I must remember to thank them again. My dear mistress, to whom I have been indentured for two years, ever since arriving in Boston on the rescue ship, is sitting close by

4

my bedside while I write. She is comforting me with words of cheer and solace.

Mr. Mather was yesterday explaining solemnly to the congregation: "The New Englanders are a people of God settled in those which were once the Devil's territories, and it may easily be supposed that the Devil was exceedingly disturbed when he perceived such a people here." How true! Mr. Mather speaks the highest truth. My own wretched circumstances bear him out. "In the horrible tempest which is now upon ourselves, the design of the Devil is to sink that happy settlement of Government wherewith the Almighty God has graciously inclined their Majesties in England to favor us." I find it comforting to copy down the notes my mistress made at yesterday's meeting.

The six men who brought me from the meeting have returned this evening to pray with me. They say I have been skipping about the house, making terrible sounds and faces. I am suddenly very tired and aching. I cannot remember the course of the day. The quill is unsteady in my hand. I must take care the inkhorn does not overturn. My tongue keeps curling in a half circle up to the roof of my mouth, not to be removed, though my mistress tries with her fingers to free it.

Now I see that short dark Devil looming Fiendishly again. He crawls toward me, reaches slyly under my gown and pinches me above the knee. I must pray.

Dec. 6

Mr. Mather urges me to write a full account of my memories, especially of past fits and seizures. When he is seated near me, or bowed down on his knees, I feel strong enough to recall those horrors without permitting them to overwhelm me. He impresses upon me, repeatedly, the importance of my journal in providing him with evidence for his noble undertaking. "I have indeed set myself," he explains to me, "to countermine the whole plot of the Devil against New England, in every branch of it, as far as one of my darkness can comprehend such a work of darkness."

But Mr. Mather is divine light itself. How blest I am to have been ransomed from Quebec by the Boston English, indeed by Mr. Mather's own church. Over the course of a year and more here in Boston I was beginning to live at peace with my memories. And then, suddenly, some six months ago, began my Hellish punishment.

What malefic influence caused my torment all at once to kindle? Was it the evil vapors coming from Salem, where Witches and Wizards were being judged and executed, according to their deserts?

Didn't the emanations of their malevolence spread even as far as Jamaica, causing an earthquake that killed thousands of islanders—all this holocaust occurring at the precise moment when I was first taken by Satanic seizures?

I cannot forget the wild sight of prisoner Sarah Good in her cell. I had heard all the accounts of her Witchery. The news of those accursed visitations upon the town of Salem were on every tongue. When she was transferred last March to our Boston jail, I could scarcely bear the delay before I might see her for myself. I needed to take a hard sharp look at her, for my own peace of mind. I had to know if Goody Good belonged to those Tawnies in whose power we children—those of us spared an early death—spent so many cruel weeks.

It seemed to me an endless year of waiting since the moment of the Witch's arrival in Boston. It was only a few months by the calendar. I longed to confront her. At last my mistress sent me on an errand near the jail. I crept in. Sure enough, she wore the filthy skin and fierce expression of our Indian tormentors. I knew for certain she was one of them.

Suddenly I was shocked almost into a faint when she called out to me as I passed: "Give me a little tobaccy, girl!"

My limbs went stiff as fire tongs, my mouth went sawdust-dry, my tongue curled and lodged in the back of my throat. I could not breathe.

I saw a yellow bird, Goody Good's familiar, sucking between her fingers that clutched the prison bars. She offered to give me such a bird for myself. Did she think I was the Devil's minion?

I fell with a loud thud to my knees. My hands landed in the wood shavings spread thick upon the floor. I seized the rough material for dear life, and threw handfuls—as though with my last breath—through the bars. *"There's* tobacco good enough for you!" I rasped. A fit of coughing doubled me up. Someone helped me to my feet and out of the prison.

This was the beginning of my attacks, half a year ago. They have continued, off and on, as the Demons choose, over the past months. Dr. Oakes has looked in on me again. He confirms the new onset of Bewitchment.

Dec. 7

I have eaten not a mouthful since the Lord's Day, three whole days ago. The Evil Spirits are once again defying me even to open my lips. It is much like my molestation of last June, when prisoner Goody Good plagued me into a fast of twelve days together. I became too weak to perform the least household tasks. My mistress berated me, until Mr. Mather, curious to examine my condition, spent a whole evening with me. He explained to her the Demonic nature of my illness. My clothes hung like a loose Indian tunic about me. I missed my monthly course.

My dear mistress, under whose roof I have lived in contented service for two years now, reminds me how blest I am in my misfortune, to be a case of deep interest to the good minister. Even in Salmon Falls we knew the name of Cotton Mather, and of his illustrious father and grandfathers.

"Mr. Mather is widely renowned," says my mistress, "for his handling of Bewitched young girls and young women. Though not directly involved in the Salem trials, his opinion has been eagerly sought and attended to."

I tell her he is a ray of light in my lair of Devilment.

It is sad that the Witchery has now returned, after several blessed free days, to punish me. Dear Mr. Mather comes often and prays long with me. On occasion neighbors join him in a day of fasting. They fast by choice, not, as in my case, by Devilish necessity. Sometimes I think I detect an Imp even in the midst of the pious company. Thus, I prefer to be prayed for by the good minister alone. Often he prostrates himself in the dust.

I have a mortal chill and tremble like a drying nightshirt in our sharp December sea-wind. And yet I burn with the fever of a brand ablaze in the fires of Hell. Mr. Mather says he will pluck me out. With God's help.

> *But oh! the torture, vomit,*
> *screechings, groans!*
> *And six weeks fever would pinch*
> *hearts like stones.*

My mistress reads to me against the Fiends. I find a wry comfort in the poems of Edward Taylor. They are like the astringent berries of the choke cherry, the size of marrow-fat peas, we children dared one another to taste. They pucker the mouth of the eater and darken the teeth and the lips. I have an appetite for bitterness.

Dec. 8

Still cannot eat.

It is like the total fast of last month, in which a broth of fresh beef smelled like horse urine, and new apple cider stung like vinegar. My mistress urges me, over and over, to take nourishment. She is a kind woman. I am glad to be in her service. My duties are no more rigorous than at home in Salmon Falls. And she instructs me in fine handiwork such as I never learned in my country childhood. Best of all, she lets me read the books in her considerable library, inherited from her late husband: mostly solemn religious writers, including the Mathers, of course. But eloquent Milton among them. Some pagan and Catholic authors, as well. And Gerard's *Herball*, my mistress's favorite. What a pity I cannot read the Greek and Latin verse.

I have an impulse to seize my mistress's hand and lick it like a devoted dog. But my tongue is parched with the memory of how we starved, between feastings, on our ragged and limping march to Quebec.

The bodies of my parents lay dead at home in Salmon Falls. Ebenezer and Deliverance perished early, but the rest of us tried to live on Tawny food those eight captive months, whenever we could find it. But there was a Devilish taste to every groundnut. I was certain each bite drove me deeper into Evil power. Acorns, purslain, hogweed, and sometimes dog's flesh. Once a bear was killed, and another time a turtle. I tasted only the smallest pieces of them; even so, I gagged on the morsels, and suffered belly pangs of guilt for living on the food of our Persecutors. An Indian gave me a slice of moose's liver, which was very sweet indeed. And we had fish, if we could catch it.

Once I was left with a squaw while the others went to look for eels. We boiled a maggoty bladder of moose and drank the broth. The bladder was so tough we could not chew it. But then the roasted eel! Never have I tasted a more savory dish. Was it right to be so well satisfied?

Mr. Mather says it was right for me to keep eating in the wilderness, even the food of the Savages. He says I should now try to eat the food offered by the kind Christians who surround me. He bids me sing a hymn line with him:

For thou shalt eat with cheer.

He does not understand that there may be a Devil among these Boston English.

But yet beware of Satan's wily baits!
He lurks among you. Cunningly he waits.

Dec. 9

Still cannot eat.

And still I remain here in this friendly house, close by Mr. Mather's church, where five days ago I fell under the spell of the Wizards anew. Mr. Mather has told me that in the midst of his sermon I sank into a swoon like death. But how do the Fiends dare enter the house of the Lord? When I awoke I was thrashing so violently in all directions with all my limbs, strong men could not carry me farther than this dwelling, where kindly neighbors took me in. They are outstanding citizens of our town. This house is filled with fine furnishings. My host's ships are in the harbor. Through the diamond windowpanes I see tall masts that were once the soaring white pines of my beloved New Hampshire.

My mistress asks me to describe my Tormentors. Like heathen they are, like the painted idols of heathen!

> *Mouths have they, speechless yet they be.*
> *Eyes have they, but they do not see.*
> *Ears have they, but they do not hear.*

13

My mistress, who lives half a mile away, comes daily to see me, and brings always some familiar tidbit with which to tempt me. I dare not open my mouth lest the Specters, always hovering near, thrust a little poisoned cup against my lips, and pour the whitish liquor down my throat. When they force too fiercely, Mr. Mather lays his hand on my mouth, and keeps me from swallowing the venom. In gratitude I kiss his palm. Then the Spectors become very agitated and scratch their nails noisily on bed and wall. Their scrapings can be heard by more than seven witnesses at a time. The raucous Fiends bid me note how Mr. Mather's sentences come out groping and uneven between his teeth.

One of the Imps hisses that I may be myself a Witch. God forbid! Let no one else hear their foul whisperings. They instruct me to feel my privy parts for an excrescence, out of which my Imp sucks nourishment during the night, and at the same time infuses me with a ferment which makes my body buoyant. They speak of the dread water-test. They laugh at my terror, and pretend to reassure me. I have only to let myself be cross-bound, they cackle, my right thumb made fast to my left great-toe and left thumb to right great-toe, and then lowered into the Bay. Surely I would not sink. Surely I would float, by my sheer Witchery, in the manner of a buoy in the harbor.

Even the pillow held against my ears cannot drown out their vexing talk. There are pins in among the feathers. They prick my cheeks and ears. Why has Mr. Mather left so early?

Dec. 10

Still cannot eat.

My mistress, surely as loving as a mother might be, quotes verses of Edward Taylor:

> *Necessity*
> *Saith I must eat this flesh,*
> *If not, no life's in me that's worth a fly:*
> *and drink this blood.*
> *This mortal life, while here,*
> *eats mortal food.*

Where am I? I do not recognize this room. Since yesterday there is a great haze all around me. Suddenly it is alive with Fiends flocking to my bed. They are forcing pins into my mouth, for me to swallow. Someone—Mr. Mather?—finally wrenches them away. Then they return and sit on my chest, so that I cannot draw breath. I am like old Giles Cory, who was pressed to death by rocks placed on his chest. Poor old Cory. He stood mute—except to cry out for more rocks laid upon him.

Am I to cry out "More weight! More weight!" Merciful Lord, am I to be pressed to death?

Mr. Mather reminds me that Giles Cory was being tried for a felony. He was obstinate before the law. The magistrates hoped he would break down under punishment and give testimony. "The sheriff," says Mr. Mather, "was merely applying the English procedure of *peine forte et dure* to a stubborn criminal. You must remember, dear Mercy, that poor young Ann Putnam suffered even more than old Giles, and on his account. Precisely at the moment when the rocks were laid on Giles's chest, a whole coven of Witches pressed in upon Ann, and crushed her chest, and choked the breath from her body, and tormented her, saying that she must be pressed to death before ever Giles was. By God's grace, she was released."

God grant me release. When Mr. Mather calls me *dear Mercy* I feel the stirrings of release.

Who's brushing my hair? Negra? It's Negra, my mistress's mulatto slave from Barbados. Her stroking touch soothes me with its gentle rhythm. She often asks to brush my hair, it is so different from her own. Hers is a nest of darkness, bristly as witches'-broom. Mine is Indian corn silk, at its most red-golden moment. Or so a tribesman once told me. His own straight locks were glossy crow-black—they felt like bird wings under my caressing hand. His eyes were black, black, deep drowning wells.

Negra's eyes are tar-black as an Indian's. Mine are hazel, green-gray with coppery cat-flecks. My infant's eyes were river-gray. I have told Negra about my infant. My mistress knows. She says I need not speak of it.

She comes toward me with a cup of cider. But a Fiend slithers between me and my wish to please her: a short dark fellow of tawny complexion, with straight hair, on top of which perches a high-crowned hat.

One foot is cloven. He brings with him a number of Specters, who obey him as their master, and taunt me with the hideous assaults to which he inspires them. I am in a dark, desolate cellar, where day is indistinguishable from night. Mr. Mather moves his hands toward my eyes, but I see right through them, they are but air, to the Hellish Harpies fluttering about the room. He lays one hand upon my eyes, to keep the Fiends from my view. But his touch so pains me, I have to pull away his wrist and bite it. His speech stammers as he sorrowfully upbraids me.

While my mistress soaks his wound in warmed water, I tear a leaf from his Bible. Thereupon, the Demons rejoice aloud, in big thick voices. I hear myself ranting along with them. My voice is as hoarse as any Devil's. Mr. Mather puts his mouth to my ear and halloos powerfully, but I cannot bear to listen to him. I have half a rash mind to bite his lip. "Haah!" I cry. Or "How!" Or "What do you say, Fiend?" Mr. Mather does not see the Devils, nor hear them, nor feel their pinching. I show him marks of innumerable pins that have been stuck in me. He cannot fail to acknowledge the bloody marks of the Witch-wounds, can he?

When the Fiend's assault I flee,
Lord, dear God, turn not from me.

Dec. 11

A crow is cawing outside my window. His black voice comes through sheets of snow which hang like rippling bedclothes in the air. A sudden sidewise flurry whips a white flock like migrating moths against the window. I long to go out and scoop up a handful of flakes to lay upon my tongue. Such a cooling apparition, the snow.

"If your bloody soul be washed in the Lord's blood," says Mr. Mather, "it shall be made whiter than the snow."

I need some sweet frosty comfort against my feverish Devilment. The Specters might not pursue me if I could escape outdoors. I am their prisoner here in this Christian house. How I ache to bathe my hot fingers in the freezing foam. To work the suds into a ball. To roll the ball downhill while it grows fuller, fuller, to the size of a snowman's body. I hear us laughing together, my sisters and brothers. One of them brings another ball, smaller, the right size for a head. Quick, someone, two black-charred embers for eyes! Ah yes, a turnip for nose. A dried bean-pod for upturned mouth. Oh, the jolly Jack Frost, dear comical creature of my childhood! Fetch a hat, someone!

No, no, not that high-crowned headpiece of my Tormentor!

The wind, the wind grows merciless. Where is our shelter? Snow lies knee-deep, my legs and hams are sore. We travel over steep and hideous mountains, then swamps and thickets of fallen trees, lying one, two, three feet from the ground. I step on them from one to another, a thousand or so in a day. My sores are bleeding, I might be tracked by the blood left behind me in the snow. Yet I must continue hurrying up and down in the wilderness, in this late northern winter, at the pace of my Demons. Or else be killed by them. Pinched with cold for lack of clothing, in the Indian dress they have foisted upon me, a thin worn deerskin, no woolen stockings, only their leather moccasins, no proper rackets for my sodden feet, which are continually pricked with sharp stones and thorny branches broken on the ground.

My life hangs hourly in doubt. Mr. Mather is too busy, this Lord's Day, to spend more than a moment here as he passes on his way to the congregation. I will sing against the darkness. A psalm, a psalm against the Sabbath doom!

Much ill our woeful eyes have seen—

Save me, Mr. Mather!

Dec. 12

More crows. My mistress has put out the bones of our Thanksgiving turkey for the birds to pick clean. She has meant to enliven my morning with their comings and goings. A week ago I tasted her turkey broth, the last nourishment I have swallowed in seven haunted days and nights. I am sickened by the sight of a shiny congregation of creatures glinting against the snow. From their perch on the limbs overhead they examine the mess of leftovers. Flapping and cawing they study the gift. Is it safe? Dare they accept it? Greedy and suspicious both, they hover like Specters over the skeleton. In their black ministerial garb they finally swoop down, then mince around the offering, not yet brave enough to approach. They leave a footprint like the *broad arrow* mark blazed by the hatchet into the tallest of our New Hampshire pines, those tree-giants reserved for the masts of the Royal Navy. How the furious birds would scold at woodsmen cutting down a favored perch! To think I once laughed at the cawings of crows, and answered them back in their own raucous voice.

One of the creatures, the most audacious, seizes a gobbet in his gross bill and soars away. The others follow, uncertainly. I know their fear. They hold down their evil feet on the ragged carcass and tear up beakfuls. They remind me of funereal Puritans bowed and chanting psalms in the meetinghouse. They are fearful of the succor availing them. They lack conviction. They are nervous as captives. I vomit a sickly thin fluid into the bowl at my bedside. Negra washes my mouth and rinses the bowl.

The Devils are assaulting me again. They rail and slander against good Mr. Mather because I quote him in my arguments defying their malignity. Mr. Mather explains their behavior. "Among those judgments of God which are a great mystery, I suppose few are more unfathomable than this, that pious and holy men suffer sometimes by the force of horrid Witchcrafts, and Hellish forces are permitted to break through the hedge which our Heavenly Father has made about them that seek Him. I suppose the instances of this direful thing are seldom, but that they are not never, we can produce very dismal testimony."

Can it be that Mr. Mather is referring to *himself* as the victim of such Devilry? No, that is impossible. He is far too saintly to be thus attacked. And so I confront the Specters and insist that yesterday he prayed for me (I think he said) no fewer than ten times, four of which were with me here. Yet the Devil sachem reviles him, and brays out against him, saying he did not pray for me yesterday so much as once. Sometimes I hardly know which voice to believe.

Dec. 13

The leaded diamonds of this windowpane are a frozen forest. Overnight these woods have come alive with icy forms. I trace the outline of a pond, and then a beaver. They were such busy animals, we often stopped to watch them on our way to Quebec. Sometimes we heard a tree crash when they had chewed it to the breaking point. Such fierce little laborers, they gave us captives cheer and courage. And the dear little kits born in spring with full coats of fur and eyes wide open! We could not bear the sight of our captors skinning the animals for their pelt. Our Boston gentlemen like to wear a good castor hat. Beavers, they say, mate for life. Shall I mate for life, ever? ~~How briefly mated once I~~

Now a moose is looming onto the panes of this frosty window. His antlers grow, they spread across the glass and leadings, over the whole width. He is coming perilously close. I smell his animal breath. His horns are Devilish headgear. Kill him, someone! Ah, that's better. ~~Strike about with your swords! No~~ matter you cannot *see* the Fiend. He is there, under his malefic cloak of invisibility. What foolish colonist would hope to domesticate the monster? Beasts of

Hell they are! Hardly to be tamed into beasts of burden.

Wolves are howling somewhere in the distance. Pray for me, Mr. Mather, never stop praying!

Staghorns! A red tongue is impaled on the branch of a sumac. Birds are pecking at it. Now the tongue moves. It is flying away! A soaring tongue! Mr. Mather says he has never before seen a cardinal bird in Boston. But I know it is the Devil's messenger. I warn you, Mr. Mather! Let me sing back to you the hymn you have taught me:

> *Cunningly he waits*
> *To catch you from me; live not then secure,*
> *But fight against sin, and let your lives be pure.*
> *Prepare to hear your sentence—*

A hand seizes my throat as though to choke me. Whose hand? Mr. Mather pulls away and prostrates himself with his face in the dust of the floor. He prays so hard his words stumble. I am glad when at last he breaks into a hymn tune. He seldom stammers in singing.

Dec. 14

The Fiend is hooting in the chimney. The flames, his fiery companions, cackle on the hearth. Mr. Mather says it is only the crackling of oak and hickory logs. Poor Mr. Mather, he cannot see we are in mortal danger. He presses me to join him in singing a sturdy psalm. Holy music shall drown out other sounds.

But look, Mr. Mather! The whole room is blackened by the smoke of Indian campfires! Is that a company of squaws I see standing about? Did you invite them to pray for me? Are they Red Christians, from Mr. John Eliot's flock? I met a praying Tawny once who told me he had a brother whose conscience was so delicate he would not eat horse. But he was robust as Hell for the slaughter of Christians. And another praying Indian was so cruel as to wear a string about his neck, strung with Christian fingers.

I love the Lord, because he doth
My voice and prayer hear,
And in my days will call because
He bowed to me his ear.

24

The pangs of death on every side
About beset me round;
The pains of Hell gat hold on me—

The sounds grate against my ears. They rasp in my throat. Mr. Mather praises the squaws. How can he suffer their voices? We hear different musics. Open your ears, Mr. Mather, while there is yet time! Hear the Savages beating drums as they dance around the pine tree! Look, a bear is dancing with them! Shoot him through the head, quick, before he hugs me to death in his great paws! Seize those Devilish boys and girls playing jokes on each other, dancing mirthfully and tingling the silvery bells sewn in their garments! How riotous the color of that clothing! How frantic the pursuit of pleasure! Bind the Heathen crew, whip the Devilry out of them! Set them in stocks, brand them, crop their ears! They are no better than Quakers! Punish the vile tribe! More whippings, more chainings, more jailings, more burnings, more hangings!

And yet the Indian children were sweet to play with. They knew the name of every plant along the path. They stroked the pussy willows with their fingertips. They were first to see the first hood of skunk cabbage poking through the leaf litter. They signaled us to watch the flies crawling into the stinking little tents and climbing the cob of flowers within. They pointed—without picking it—to the fragile bloom of bloodroot, the clear white petals radiating from the golden center. As evening closed it, they showed us how the bloom itself closes, how the single, irregular leaf wraps protectively around the flower stalk. They even dared us to taste the milky, acrid, orange sap.

How they laughed at us then!

We laughed together at jack-in-the-pulpit, a heathenish laugh at the comical little preacher, whose English name we explained to the coppery little heathen. They pronounced the syllables distinctly.

And the moccasin flower! How proud I was to be the first to see it, one day late in May, two months into the march. Like a swift forest brook it was, a fall of freshets, delicate pink foam rippling down a slope of gravelly woodland! How royally the little pink pouch preens itself, dangling at the top of its stem! How the wild bee seeks it out, not to be denied! For a moment I could believe myself buoyant as the showy creature herself. Within me I could feel the pollen from the back of the visiting honey-gatherer rub off upon my hidden stigmata.

The little Tawnies were first to see the thaw-butterfly. I followed it where it rested its purple-brown wings of velvet edged with straw-gold. It drank at the sap oozing out of bruised tree-bark. They bade us feel for ourselves how sticky were the plump and polished horse chestnut buds. They pointed to the new pale gold under the ravaged sycamore skins, a first brave sun glimpsed through breaking clouds. Dear Lord, let me feel some new hope of light shining through my ragged griefs and losses!

One of the children taught us how to make a little *pishing* sound, a way to bring birds out of hiding, to satisfy our curiosity. They warned us of wasps' nests, and the pairs of spines jutting from the prickly ash, which our New Hampshire neighbors called wait-a-bit, how rightly. When I suffered toothache, a beautiful black-eyed boy tore a piece of smooth silvery bark and showed me how to chew it. I chewed purposefully. But even more intently I watched the strange sleeping forms which now lay exposed to the cold, their coverlet ripped away. A mass of hibernating spiders among their young; drowsy triangular moths; anglewing butterflies resembling dead engraved beetles in their delicate carvings. How little we know what lies concealed from us in this world, from the witness of our eyes. But nature's is not a malign invisibility.

When I told Mr. Mather that tooth pain left me within the hour, he reminded me that toothache is a sign one has sinned with one's teeth. Do I detect him smiling as he goes on? "So then, there are fifty-two Tormentors in your gums alone, twenty milk teeth to begin with, to which your sin has made you liable, as in the course of your life they may arise and appear and corrupt; and the nerve at the bottom of each becomes uneasy." No, I am mistaken, he is certainly *not* smiling. He continues solemnly: "The teeth wherein I suffer so much torture—how much have I *sinned* with them! The sin of my first parents, Adam and Eve, was perpetrated by the teeth. A horrid sin, a sin that is mine and forever to be bewailed."

I keep on writing as swiftly as Mr. Mather talks. It behooves me to keep these admonitions of his always close at hand. He borrows my note-takings only briefly, to copy whatever is significant into his own journal.

About the sins of the mouth there is more to come. "You have employed your teeth in eating irregularly, inordinately, and without a due regard for the service and glory of God in your eating."

But on the march, I tell him, I was forced to eat irregularly, and sometimes inordinately. Mr. Mather sweeps aside my protest. "How often have I dug my grave with my teeth. And how justly am I punished with pains in the teeth, which have been so abused! My teeth are used in my speech. Some of the letters pronounced in speaking are the dentals. In speaking amiss, how many sins have I been guilty of!"

Could that be the reason for his stumbling, sometimes, in his speech?

I found myself quite exhausted with writing down at fever speed the wise observations of our minister. At least his deliberate delivery is slower than might be. I dropped my pen and lay idle, resting, while he continued with many practical recommendations for the relief of toothache. My mistress has taken notes. I recover strength enough, presently, to make brief jottings: thighbone of a toad; bowels of a sow bug; bethany thrust up the nose. And if there's nothing else to be done, draw the tooth.

Everyone knows about Thomas Parker, the celibate, sweet-voiced singer who retains his excellent voice until very old age because his teeth hold sound and good until then. It's his custom to wash his mouth and rub his teeth every morning.

I wonder if sassafras leaves are a sin? I remember we picked them at the perfect moment for chewing, small and tender and green as a darner.

Dec. 15

Still another memory: The Redskins were first to hear the geese going over toward their northern home. Our captors pointed upwards with fingers fitted into a V. We followed with our eyes the direction of their pointing, but our thoughts flew south. We could not laugh with the children, nor even smile with the old ones. Mr. Roger Williams's sweet hymn hums sadly in my ears:

> *The very Indian boys can give*
> *To many stars their name,*
> *And know their course and therein do*
> *Excel the English tame.*

But not Mr. Mather, they don't excel *him.* He has often looked through a telescope. He claims that our earth is but as a pin's point compared with God's mighty universe. Were we among the stars, we should utterly lose sight of our globe. Even more astonishing, he has seen with the aid of a microscope myriad magnified animals, of which many hundreds would equal a grain of sand. How exquisite, how stupendous must be the structural greatness of the little things which our naked eyes cannot penetrate into.

"There is not a fly," says Mr. Mather, "but what may confuse an atheist."

As for confusion, there are scores of God's creatures to trouble a Christian. I think of fleas, mites, mosquitoes, blood-suckers, that prolific and hostile crew. Their vexations outweigh their astonishments. And bees, beautiful, useful, talented, industrious as they are, their stings are no laughing matter. Nor the poisonous ivy, which like a leering Fiend invites us to gather its autumn fire. Villainous is the rash that follows.

Dec. 16

Oh but we had to laugh at the first boasting songs of frogs! It was the Tawny children hushed us into listening. As soon as the air began to warm, and the woodland pools melted, we could see a peeper posing on a floating twig, his swollen throat shining like a great white bubble bigger than himself. At first a hesitant, impure peep as he warms up; then the true, strong, assured whistle. Other bubble-throated creatures sang with him, but they disappeared all together into the water at the least rustle not of their own making. They stayed hidden among the sodden floating leaves. Later, they sang more courageously at dusk, and all through the night.

The shaking of sleighbells passing my window brings back those nights of our capture. The season was turning summer, but the air was winter-white with snow-music. Here in this bitter month I still smell that sweetening time, when my nose trembled at the scent of wet, warming soil under pulpy logs. Bending to a cluster of dead dry stalks, I broke open the little low jar at the top of the stem. Snuff-brown seed-dust spilled out of the old Indian pipe into my palm. Then I searched for new pipes, white as maggots. I dreamed of spring in Salmon Falls, and the chalky rills in the bubbling river.

How silently the Tawnies glided in their canoes. Their paddles never lifted out of the water. I felt like a fish lying in the bottom of the boat. And yet I could breathe the sweet air into my lungs, though all around me and under me I heard the *slap slap* of the current against the birch hull. Once we came to a river swelled high with spring freshets. The swift stream was terrifying. Our sachem paddled about one hundred yards up the creek by the shore side, turned into the raging current, and steered us onto the other side as accurately as an arrow shot out of the bow by a strong arm. The Redskins are beautiful as statues when they stand poised with bow and arrow.

They are fearful as Demons when they raise a musket.

Dec. 17

This morning, thinking of spring freshets, I ask for a little sip of cold water for my craving stomach. I am at once thrown into hideous torments, as the Fiends force their pitchforks into my very bowels. I throw my arms around Mr. Mather, begging him to help me out of my torture. Sing, Mr. Mather, sing!

> *Let Him with kisses of His mouth*
> *Be pleased me to kiss,*
> *Because much better than the wine*
> *Thy lovingkindness is.*

> *Thy name as poured forth ointment is,*
> *Because of the sweet smell*
> *Of Thy good ointments, therefore do*
> *The virgins love Thee well.*

I am so weak, I have scarcely embraced Mr. Mather, when I fall back into a faint. He revives me with a cold compress and stammering prayers. I cry out, raving, that I shall die for lack of food. He comforts me with telling the case of Rebecca Smith who, Bewitched, continued without eating or drinking for ten weeks together, and afterwards lived only upon warm broths taken in small quantities for a whole twelve-month. Long fasting, he says, is not only feasible but strangely agreeable to such as have something more than ordinary to do with the invisible world.

I cannot believe the good minister. I shall not survive this Bewitchment. He is too trusting. I tell him he has been reading false reports. I cannot persuade him how grave my misery has become. He is certain he is stronger, with God's help, than the Fiend. Why, then, do his words stumble against one another as he pleads with the Lord for my deliverance? Why did not God long since extinguish the Devil that made all men and women so bad, God having all power? I know I shall not live out the year in this Hellish famine.

A smell like frosty evenings on the march to Quebec. Chestnuts are roasting on the hearth. Their snapping merriment reminds me of winter evenings by the hearth in Salmon Falls. When I ask for one, Mr. Mather peels it for me. Why do his hands tremble? For his sake I will survive against the Fiend.

A silence is ringing in my ears. I lie back against the bolster and listen. The nine o'clock bell ringing out from the meetinghouse. Then a short bark ending in a snarl. A fox is hunting in the night. What a foolish story a garrulous neighbor is telling us. And yet the hushed company gathered about my bed listens with attention to the tale of one Rosalie who lived for forty days on air sipped from a spoon.

Dec. 18

The Lord's Day again, and I can expect very little of Mr. Mather's attention to my needs. Oh yes, he will pray for me with the congregation in the meeting-house. But I mean right here beside my bed. At my bedside is where his prayers most affect me. My mistress promises to take notes on the sermon and read them to me. I hope writing in this journal for Mr. Mather will help pass the day. He has already praised my fluent accounts, more than once. My skill is not surprising, I told him. My father, an esteemed and honest man, taught us children to write at an early age. Busy though he was with his fields and animal husbandry and lumbering, yet he encouraged us to study the written word. Often he quoted John Robinson, the Pilgrim pastor in Holland. In that famous farewell sermon before departure for these shores, Mr. Robinson told his flock: "It is not possible that the full perfection of knowledge should break forth at once. Therefore folk must examine the written word and compare it and take care what they receive for truth."

I must reread what I have been writing. I hope no

35

errors of grammar or spelling have crept in. How many spelling-bees I have won in Salmon Falls!

Negra keeps faithful watch over me, warming my bed with a stone at my feet. I lie in comfort here. This fine house is well furnished with china, pewter, tall chests of drawers, a wall clock, silver tankards on the sideboard. I should be content. Periwigged portraits on the wall. Rich food in abundance, good Madeira, none of which I can abide. I am without hope or desire for my life.

Outside, sheet after sheet of snow, a white smother. White as the skinned legs of clownish frogs we roasted over open fires. The Indian children were quick to catch the creatures in their hands. We tried to learn, but lost the slippery stuff as often as we seized at it. I refused at first to taste the skinned flesh. But hunger won against me. The little roasted drumsticks were finer than young poultry. I ate more than my share. Then I grew sick, and puked, and was laughed at.

I hear a laughter on the hearth. Someone is hissing, and a mist is rising like morning veils over the pond. The Devil, look at him, is a Great Frog! There he is, coming down the flue! Over there, beyond the lug-pole, stepping into the warming-pans, cracking and grating! Look! At the mouth of the chimney! He's pulling apart the pot-chains and trammels, knocking the pots and skillets to the hearth floor, spilling the curdling milk! Oh, we were safer under the skies in our capture!

Now I see, it's a Witch's teat, swollen into a frog-bubble. Let it burst! Let the power of the Devil burst its own poison-sac! Stay away from here, Mr. Mather, this evil Lord's Day! Those somber spots are plague signs. This house is marked for destruction. Mr. Wigglesworth has written the awful sentence:

> *Earth is to me a prison;*
> *This body an useless weight.*

Those little Tawny bodies, how freely, how weightlessly they chased and played with us, as though they were our own brothers and sisters. Some of them were cousin to my infant. We grew familiar with their lovely bronze bodies. I grew all too strangely familiar with one splendent bronze body.

The native children called our attention to the meadow frog, which they hailed as the most beautiful of all. And so it was, slender, smooth-skinned, green or brown, with that light stripe running from each eye back along the sides. We never found two creatures to match, so delicately varied were their patterns.

Yet the Devil can work his Wizardry on the most innocent, the most precious of God's creatures, animal and human. And therefore we must take care whom we cry out against. Mr. Mather warns me, from time to time, that this is a counsel I must never fail to remember. "I cannot warn you," he says, "too emphatically. I had rather judge a Witch to be an honest woman than an honest woman to be a Witch."

Shall I not despise the serpent in Eden?

Some of my questions Mr. Mather deems foolish. Has Mr. Mather himself ever been cried out against? My mistress reports that some of the Salem folk may have been unjustly accused, and then were hanged. Let God spare all honest Christians.

The snow is turning into a mizzling rain. No Specters now in sight. I reach out and pick an apple from the bowl. I bite into it uncertainly. It smells of October in New Hampshire. But there is a worm on my tongue. I spit out.

Everyone at the Lord's Day sermon. Even Negra. They have decided I can be left alone, at least for the length of the service. Especially since they will be praying hard for me. The house is empty and haunted. They are hoping to make a Christian of Negra. I wonder. Negra says a company of poor Negroes asked Mr. Mather to organize a special society for the welfare of their miserable nation that were servants among us. She attended one of the meetings. Mr. Mather preached to them on the sixty-eighth psalm: *Princes shall come out of Egypt; Ethiopia shall soon stretch out her hands unto God.* "But what about Barbados?" says my dear Negra.

She has shown me a list which Mr. Mather drew up for the society. We have sighed together over the series of eight rules. Members are obliged never to meet without leave of such as have power over them, and to meet only with people who have sensibly reformed their lives. Members should invite good English neighbors, including preachers, to visit them and do what they think is fitting for the Negroes. Members should admonish and, in extreme cases, exclude fellow members who steal, swear, lie, fornicate, drink excessively, or disobey their masters. No shelter is to be given to runaways. Owners should be informed of any member who had pretended to come to a meeting but had instead gone elsewhere.

I have explained to Negra that the moment a Negro is missing from the town, you have only to notify the Savages, who, provided you promise them something and describe the man or woman to them, will find the poor creature right soon. Says Negra: "I doubt I'll ever turn into a good Christian."

Mr. Mather has left behind a book he was consulting on my behalf. The page turns to a girl my age. Mr. Duke's daughter became ill in July of 1684. I must copy out her history. Perhaps it will bring comfort to mine.

She fell into a total suppression of her monthly courses from a multitude of cares and passions of her mind, but without any symptom of the green sickness following upon it. From which time her appetite began to abate, and her digestion to be bad; her flesh also began to be flaccid and loose, and her looks pale. I do not remember that I did ever in all my practice see one that was conversant with the living so much wasted (like a skeleton only clad with skin) yet there was no fever, but on the contrary a coldness of the whole body, with fainting fits, which did frequently return upon her.

Help me! Help me! Can no one hear? I am screaming for help! For hours I am screaming!

At last the door bursts open.

Dec. 19

Mr. Mather urges me to eat. He holds out an apple. I pick up a knife and ask him to cut the fruit in half. The cut meat smells warm and cool at once. I offer him the other half of white flesh.

The Demons still plague me, but today their pitchforks feel less pointed. Loud voices are coursing through my head. Some of them say, "Eat, eat, eat!" Others say, "Don't, don't, don't!" They all cry out Satanically. In the room overhead someone is stomping like a crazed monster. On the trail we marveled how the Indians moved swiftly and stealthily. Why do they now change from moccasins to boots? Here comes a Tawny descending the stairs like the tread of doom. But I will speak out to him with a great voice.

"Horrid wretch!" I cry. "You make my very heart cold within me! It is Hell to me, to hear you speak! Don't assault me any longer with vile blasphemies! You are a beast! I think truly that hogs are fittest company for you! You pretend you love me, hah! Then why do you continue to starve me? It is fifteen days since I have eaten decent victuals! I'll faint dead away before ever I reach my next birthday, before I am betrothed, even! How should I know to whom? Oh, listen to you, such fine promises! You'll bestow a husband on me if I'll be your servant? What! Is my life in your hands? No, if it were, you would have killed me long before this hour. Well, if you do burn me, I had better burn for an hour or two here, than in Hell forever. What's that? Will you burn all Boston and shall I be burned in that fire? No, Fiend, never! It is not in your power! God and Mr. Mather will see to that!''

And I roared out the couplet at him:

> What! is a scar-fire broken out? No, no.
> The bells would backward ring if it was so.

Now I see the lips of the church company, half a hundred of them here by my bedside, moving as though in prayer; but I cannot hear the sounds. And yet I just heard the cry of a babe in a young girl's arms. I wish I had my babe in arms. Let me comfort my baby!

Dr. Oakes examines me and prescribes a plug of Negro wool in my ears, against the deafness, noises and ringings. My mistress cuts off two small tufts from Negra's head.

Strangely, I am not certain, now that I have written down my challenge to the Devil, that I did speak the words aloud. Sometimes a stone lodges on my tongue, and a pebble in each ear. A bunch, like a pullet's egg, rises in my throat, ready to choke me. Birds are sorely pecking at my earlobes, pricking them.

Hush! A black-clad cricket is chirping near the chimney, safe out of the cold. He cheered us through those long, warm northern nights. I tell Mr. Mather the creature will bring this house God's blessing. But the good minister goes to the hearth and crushes the small thing underfoot.

"Superstition! Devil's work!"

Why did not God give all men good hearts? I am too weary to follow Mr. Mather's argument.

Dec. 20

Last night a fire broke out in Boston. I was not surprised. I know the workings of the Fiend. And I had had warning. But help came promptly, and the blaze was contained.

Today Mr. Mather led a special prayer of thanksgiving with the neighbors gathered in this house. He reminded us that his father, beloved Mr. Increase Mather, had prophesied the great fire of '76, which would make desolate a whole portion of our town.

And so it did happen, sixteen years ago. Before daybreak the next morning, a tailor's apprentice failed to take proper notice of his candles. Rising alone and early to work, he fell asleep and let his light fire the house, which gave fire to the next, and then the next, so that about fifty landlords were despoiled of their housing. The greatest fire of our Massachusetts Bay, in all its history until that time, raged throughout the North end of Boston. Even Charlestown, on the other side of the river, was threatened by falling ash, so strong was the southeast wind that blew and magnified the flames and sparks. The Mather church, in North Square, the very meetinghouse where the congregation had listened to the forewarning, was

43

burned to the ground. And the Mather house nearby, and many precious books. A steady rain providentially prevented worse loss.

And then three years later occurred the most woeful desolation that Boston ever saw. The flames had begun at the Three Mariners tavern on the south side. Eighty-odd dwellings and all the seventy-odd warehouses with several vessels and their lading at the dock, were consumed to ashes. But in spite of conflagrations, says Mr. Mather, and to the glory of religion and the credit of the town, we now have four churches among us.

Ladders hang on the outside, for ready use in case of fire. Whoever takes one away unlawfully is fined twenty shillings. Every household keeps in readiness a filled pipe or hogshead. My mistress has at hand a twelve-foot pole with a good large swob at the end of it, to reach to the roof. And of course buckets aplenty. Town-appointed sweeps inspect our chimneys regularly. And there's a fine modern fire engine, they say the most up-to-date equipment available, managed by a dozen townsmen. At nine o'clock curfew all hearthfires must be covered or put out until half past four in the morning. The watchmen go the rounds all night until the reveille. I have nothing to fear.

Yet it was only last year that many private dwellings were lost in a fire on Mill Creek, between the drawbridge on North Street and the mill bridge on Hanover Street. Catted chimneys are a special hazard, with their plaster and lath construction.

Everyone knows there is an ordinance forbidding any further building of wooden structures, though exceptions still continue to be made. Stone or brick is recommended, with slate or tile covering. I have

44

often gone on errands to the Feather Store, on Dock Street near the head of North Street. Erected immediately after the Great Fire, it has a strong durable cement covering inserted with many fragments of gravel and broken glass. One can catch glimpses of the sharp corners of shattered dark-colored junk-bottles.

I tremble to think how violently this frame dwelling, handsome as it is, could be consumed to an ash, with myself helpless in the center of it. There is nothing more terrifying than the prospect of burning to death. But I have been reproached, and urged to dwell on less earthly concerns.

"Think heavenly thoughts," says Mr. Mather. "Attend to Michael Wigglesworth's cautionary couplet."

Impossible to forget it:

> *Thou art a pilgrim here;*
> *This world is not thy home.*

"Have I told you," asks Mr. Mather, "that Michael Wigglesworth was born in England of godly parents who lived in a wicked village? They moved away, and then God destroyed the village by fire. Mr. Wigglesworth never forgot the divine lesson. All his life here in Massachusetts he preached the dangers of fleshly lusts."

Indeed yes, I have heard all about *that.* As a tutor at Harvard College the strenuous gentleman reproved the students for playing music, for singing any tunes but the hymn tunes. Laughter and merriment were pronounced evil. What a howling wilderness of fiery sin his poems hold up for our edification!

I wonder, if a person should be encased in iron a

foot thick and thrown into the fire, what would become of his soul? I doubt the soul could come forth safely. I am more fearful of fire than of anything else in the world. Unless it be the smallpox. Nearly a thousand persons died in the last visitation. Mr. Mather says there was never such a time in Boston as during the epidemic of '78. Coffins crossing each other, bells tolling for Sabbath burial from sunrise until long after sunset. I dare not think about the ravaging disease. My throat is ablaze. I ask my mistress for a cup of cold broth, yet the soreness persists like a blade sawing. Dr. Oakes is called in to examine me. He prescribes a gargle of boy's urine. I heal with miraculous speed before the remedy arrives to be tasted.

Dec. 21

At a town in Germany, says Mr. Mather, a Demon appearing on the top of a chimney threatened that he would get the town on fire, and at length scattering some ashes about, presently burned the whole town horribly to the ground. I have attended one of Mr. Mather's Thursday lectures upon the awful subject of Eternal Burnings. He assures us that earthly incinerations can't compare with 'em.

I saw with my own eyes the burning of our dwelling in Salmon Falls. The Tawnies brought flax and hemp out of the barn, and fired the house, Satan's minions that they were. How innocently we had said our prayers, my parents and the seven of us children. How sweetly and without suspicion we slept through the night. Lying hidden in the forest that bordered the farms and clearings of Salmon Falls, the enemy waited, then made their way, through snow and ice and storm of an exceptionally prolonged winter. How secure we felt. Winter, we thought, was on our side. No one kept watch, either in fort or in house. With no knowledge or resistance on our part, the enemy easily took possession of the fort. Our men were unable to get together in a body to oppose them. In our house we held fast the door, but it was quickly broken through.

What a solemn sight, then, so many Christians falling down among bullets, spears and hatchets, and lying in their blood, some here and some there, like a company of sheep torn by wolves. All of them stript naked by a mob of Hell-hounds, roaring, ranting, chanting, dancing and whooping Demonically. A hundred English colonists were taken captive or barbarously mangled to their death. Even nursing infants were not spared.

Sometimes on the march I carried a papoose, to relieve the mother of her burden. I could almost be persuaded that Indian babes are born innocent, for there is no Evil in their faces, only a deep dark beauty.

More pearl'd within than to the seeing—

as the Dutch Christmas hymn sings praise. Surely it is only in their later years that Indians develop into Devils and become accursed-looking. Can it be that Godliness dwells even in the meanest infant?

This Prince, do they desire to find him?
They're worn-out swaddling clothes that bind him.

I was singing to my papoose one of our Bay Psalm hymns—

God set us here despite the savage world—

when suddenly an Indian came up to us with a basket of horse liver. I asked him to give me a piece.

"What!" says he. "Would you eat horse liver?"

48

I said yes, if he would give it to me, which he did. I laid it on the coals to roast, but before it was half cooked, someone snatched a portion of it away from me. I was forced to seize what remained and eat it as it was, with the blood dripping about my mouth. And yet it was a savory morsel to me in my hunger. How the bitterest thing can taste sweet in its time! Now while I sip small spoonfuls of the milky porridge my mistress has prepared for me, I describe to her a wondrous pancake of parched wheat, beaten and fried in bear's grease. I never tasted pleasanter nourishment in my life.

Dec. 22

My mistress does not like the taste of groundnuts. I disagree. She has not feasted on the tubers prepared Indian-fashion. I enjoy regaling her with tales of Indian customs, the agreeable sort. She is surprised to learn from me that hot water will boil and food will cook in a pot made of fresh bark of the birch tree. Suspended over a fire, the container boils the groundnuts, lately gathered, into a savory dry meal much like potato, though with a more nutty flavor. We spread them with raccoon's fat or with a piece of bear meat. I think if I could eat such a dish now, outdoors under the sky, I might speed my recovery from this disease of near-famine. My mistress assures me I shall soon enjoy a hearty pork stew. We shall see.

I remember how, on the march, a young woman from our village grew sickly soon after her child was born. Her milk dried up, and the sachem squaw taught her to beat walnut kernels and water to a milk, and boil with very fine ground cornmeal. The newborn babe began to thrive as though still at the breast.

I held my infant and fed it the walnut milk.

I miss my murdered brother and sister. I miss Richard, the only one of us children detained in Canada. Is he a converted French Catholic by now? Praise God the rest of us are safe here in Boston.

A converted squaw once told me that had the English been as careful to instruct her in our faith as the French were to instruct her in theirs, she might have become one of our religion. My mistress is interested in everything I tell her about the Indians. "Put it down," she urges. "Put it all down in the journal." But Mr. Mather may hold otherwise.

I am content enough to recall and set down the happy hours. These cottony clumps of snow falling past my window remind me of the corn we used to put among hot embers, stirring it without letting it burn, until it was turned almost inside out, and white and chewy. Once we poured hot maple syrup over it. We called it *snow food.*

How we savored the sweet roots of the yellow pond lily, tasty as the liver of a sheep! We let the busy muskrats, fond of the roots as we ourselves were, gather and store the plants in their notable houses of earth and sticks. Then we raided their stores. Always, though, we left a supply for the muskrats' own use. The moose deer, as well, feed upon the pond lily, at which time the Indians kill them, when their heads are under water. Raw and cooked, the roots of the cattail nourished us. We waded barefoot into the mud of shallow ponds and backwaters to collect spring shoots of the marsh marigold. And we gathered Solomon's seal, and jack-in-the-pulpit, and Turk's-cap lily. The beautiful face of nature became our nourishment. How eloquently Edward Taylor praises that lovely face!

The slips here planted, gay and glorious grow:
  Unless an Hellish breath do singe their plumes.
Here primrose, cowslips, roses, lilies blow,
  With violets and pinks that void perfumes:
  Whose beauteous leaves are lac'd with honey dew,
  And chanting birds chirp out sweet music true.

How close and devoted is the poet's kinship with nature! He could be brother to the Redskins. But the images of the poem deal, more deeply, with wedlock and the death of children. I know nothing of the one, something of the other. The poem pursues its haunting theme:

When in this knot I planted was, my stock
  Soon knotted, and a manly flower out brake.

That is to say, a man-child was born. Born into this burgeoning wedlock. *A manly flower out brake.* I cannot send the line out of my head. My poor little manly flower.

All of these wonders, says Mr. Mather, attest to God. There are no insignificant manifestations in nature. I should therefore pay most earnest attention to natural phenomena. Of course, Mr. Mather is especially concerned with *human* manifestations. There are no insignificant acts in life. "Whether one chooses a vocation or a slave, God's guidance is necessary." I ask my mistress if she had God's guidance in the buying of Negra. I must have startled her. She overturned a loblolly pot she was stirring. She very nearly scalded herself. I offered to help her.

"No, Mercy, just be quiet. Don't chatter so much." Very well. Though I thought I was entertaining her while she bent over the iron cauldron.

52

It is strange how sometimes, though not often, I seem to push her into the oven, no better than a Witch.

I have been growing hungry as I write, hungrier than an Indian papoose. To my amazement, I can scarcely wait for the mashed pumpkin my mistress is preparing. How clearly I recall an Indian pumpkin picnic under the full harvest moon. The great orange globes, vivid as the moon itself, were cut in chunks, and freed of their stringy pulp and seeds, then simply stewed in water—the less the better—without salt, butter, or spice of any sort, in pots covered with large pumpkin leaves. Our seat and table were the bare ground, our spoons were seashells, with which we sipped the warm broth. And our plates were the brilliant autumn leaves. We had no need to wash or preserve them.

This mashed pumpkin my mistress has prepared tastes sweet indeed, light, wholesome, refreshing. A little salt makes it even more savory than the Indian dish. She pours me a cup of beer. There is always good wine and beer in Puritan houses. I shall mend from this day forth.

Dec. 23

Once I went into a wigwam and saw an Indian boiling horsefeet. They eat the flesh first, and when the feet are old and dried, and they have nothing else, they cut off the feet and use them. I asked him to give me a little of his broth. He took a dish, and gave me one spoonful of samp, and bid me take as much of the boiling liquid as I wished. The taste revived me. The Indian then gave me a piece of the ruff, or riddling, of the small guts. I broiled it on the coals, and I could say with Jonathan: *See, I pray you, how mine eyes have been enlightened, because I tasted a little of this honey.* 1 SAMUEL 14:20

A slight thaw today. This week's rain and sun have melted the ways as if it were March. My hair has lost its shine. It is dull and dusty as a patch of old cornstalks. The house feels too warm. The air indoors is oppressive. My clothes are stifling. My whole body aches and itches with the need to be bathed and refreshed. The Cold Moon is waning. I have already missed the December geminids we loved to watch on clear New Hampshire nights. This imprisonment begins to punish me beyond endurance. How much longer, I wonder, before I may tear off these stinking garments? I complain to my mistress that the Fiends are Bedevilling me with a craving to strip away my clothing and stand naked, scratching myself all over my body until I draw blood.

"You fret too much, Mercy," she rejoins. "This is but a minor matter. Like the bewitchment of the cream—remember?—so that the butter would not come. You never gave me a proper explanation. The maid probably ate up the cream."

I feel my cheeks flush hot. I answer on the spur: "Or the goodwife has already sold the cream in the market!"

I have spoken insolently, and I ask her pardon. She laughs at my abject apology, and bids Negra sponge my skin where it is most irritated. The Tawnies had a comforting fir balsam which they burned in a clam-shell till of consistence like a salve. We applied it to sore feet and ankles.

On the march, we children welcomed the warm spring days by leaping into the nearest stream. We hid in the bushes while our clothes hung drying on a branch.

We chanted an Algonkian chant the Indians taught us:

> *Too many months the snow*
> *   has suffocated the earth.*
> *We are sick of the wigwams*
> *   and the smoky smell of our hair.*
> *Our clothes are full of vermin*
> *   and the stink of bear grease on our bodies.*
> *We long for the sun on our naked skin,*
> *   and grass on the naked ground.*

A young squaw explained the poem to me in her language, and then rendered it in her halting English. I have made an English chant of it. I can sing it to a psalm tune. But when Mr. Mather heard me fitting the words of Indian longing to our solemn music, he interrupted me quite fiercely. I wish he had not done so. I think the Tawnies took offense. They came bearing down upon me for the first time in many hours. There had been almost a peace between us. I pray for truce. Oh for a peace pipe! A pipe was always the first Indian courtesy offered to a guest or a stranger. I long for the smell of tobacco. Some of the tribal ceremonies, though so different from our own, were very comforting. And the Savages' contentment often found its way into our own hearts.

One of the captives once asked a sannup to explain the Algonkian religion. The warrior said: "Our people bow to the sun when it rises in the morning. We can watch it on its journey across the sky. We know what it can do for us, and what it cannot do. Your people worship a god whom they cannot even see. You don't know what he can do and what he can't do. Which is the better way?"

I pray for truce. A peace pipe would be welcome.

Dec. 24

To begin with, some hard words from Mr. Mather about yesterday's entry. The religion of the Indians is of no importance in the matter of my rescue from Bewitchment.

I must be alone again tomorrow, which is Christmas and the Lord's Day, both. Not that there will be any revelry to mark the holiday. That would be popish flummery. Everyone else will be at the meetinghouse. Though I protest that I feel well enough, Dr. Oakes advises against my going. The Devil might be there, lying in wait for me. The Devil is drawn to the meetinghouse for his cruelest attacks. My mistress promises to take notes on the sermon so that she may relate it to me.

Every Sunday evening, Mr. Mather entertains neighbors in his study with prayers and psalms and portions of the day's sermon. Sometimes it is the Young Men's Association who meet with him for evening services and religious discussion. This house feels more like a prison than ever. I begin to understand how Sarah Good must have suffered behind those bars.

To pass the Sabbath profitably, I have been given

a copy of Mr. Mather's account concerning another Witchcraft in this town, the case of the Goodwin children. Perhaps it will help me. He proposes that I sing aloud to myself some cheerful hymns from the *Bay Psalm Book.* In the loneliest hour I might even compose a spiritual song of my own. "For when I sit alone," Mr. Mather explains, "in my languishments, unable to write or to read, I often compose little hymns, and sing them unto the Lord. And even when I walk alone in the fields, in solitary places, in meditation, soliloquy and prayer, in converse with God, I find it comforts me, at such times, to sing forth my contemplations."

I cannot think of Mr. Mather in languishments.

"While I was lying on the couch," he goes on, "in the dark of the evening, I extempore composed the following hymn, which I then sang unto the Lord:

> *I will not any creature love*
> *But in the love of Thee above.*

And so on and so on. He says he designed rather *piety* than *poetry* in these lines. I find no cause to disagree.

Over and over and over Mr. Mather praises the goodness of God unto him, a vile worm, in that the Lord employs him in His ministry. It *is* a paradox.

And yet I cannot picture Mr. Mather as a vile worm. Nor as emptying the cistern of nature, making water at the wall. Negra has told me a story current in the town, of a dog coming beside Mr. Mather on such an occasion, and performing the identical act. Mr. Mather was heard to expostulate: "What mean, vile things we are, after all."

When we are not singing, or praying, or discussing the antics of the Fiends, Mr. Mather often asks me about the months on the march to Quebec. I have told him how the Indians could suffer hunger for days at a time with no complaint. We weakling English envied them their fortitude. They do not have to pause often to break their fast. But I know it is not praise of the Indians that Mr. Mather wishes me to record. Moreover, he is an accomplished faster himself, doubtless the equal of any Indian.

Today I related what I know about the little creature called a muskrat, which lives in shallow ponds where it builds sturdy houses of earth and sticks, like mole hills, and feeds on the aromatic sweet flag. It has a strong scent of musk in the month of May. Wrapped in cotton wool, the cods are very good to lay among clothes. The month of May is the preferred time to kill the rats, for then their cods have the strongest scent. This animal is not known in England. Mr. Mather likes to talk about his correspondence with scientists in foreign countries. He writes to them about the specialties of our New World: the moose, the sea-lion, the water-dove, the wild turkey, the eagle. And the hummingbirds, little wonders of our land, the least of all things that are clothed with feathers.

I thought it would interest Mr. Mather that one of our Indians could handle a rattlesnake without danger by first anointing himself with the fat of a kite, the bird which kills and eats rattlesnakes. Mr. Mather waved this report aside. He went on with tales of the boneless and toothless sharks which fishermen catch, off Cape Cod, for the oil in their liver. I have seen the oil myself, and tasted its disagreeable flavor when Dr. Oakes prescribed it. And I have seen the vast flocks of pigeons, sometimes thousands in a flock, here in Massachusetts Bay. A single flock can cover the best part of a mile. One of Mr. Mather's neighbors brought down a dozen with a single shot. Farmers feed them to hogs. Mr. Mather says cock pigeons care for the young part of the day, hen pigeons for the other.

I am not certain I believe that two men going by boat from Milford to Brainford, Connecticut, saw a *merman* about five or six feet long, with hairy face and arms. In our own village of Salmon Falls Mary Hurtado had a tale to tell about Devilish river apparitions. She and her husband were paddling in a canoe over the river when they saw an object like the head of a man new-shorn, and then about two or three feet distant from the canoe, the tail of a white cat swimming. But there was not a body visible to join head and tail together. I have heard Mr. Mather tell of the remains of a dragon over one hundred feet long from head to foot, found near the falls of James River, Virginia. Does he really believe this? And he has reported the discovery of the teeth and bones of a giant found near Claverack, thirty miles from Albany. I can sooner believe in Witches. And the Devil. Of the Devil, I have no doubt.

Devil or no, I hope I shall be going home to my mistress before the month is ended. Indeed, there is now hardly reason enough for me to stay here in this house one day longer, except that it is near our North Church, and thus convenient for Mr. Mather. He continues to visit me, although not so often as in earlier weeks. And frequently he leaves me in the company and charge of neighbors gathered to pray with me. Sometimes it is a group of young women and girls, a cheerful choir. They ask all sorts of questions about the Fiend. Is he tall? Fair of face? Does he lay his hand on me? Where? Have I felt his lips? On which part of my body?

Less often, it is a handsome chorus of young men. They ask no questions. But they sing like mighty angels. The men do not visit at the same hour as the women. Why not? After all, this is not the meeting-house, where there is a men's side and men's stairs, and a women's side and women's stairs. I remember our Indian men and women often sang together in their huts or outdoors under the sky. And sometimes they danced together. A pleasant, lively custom.

Mr. Mather has declared himself opposed to mixed dancing, indeed to dancing at all. Several times in the past, dancing-masters have attempted to open schools of instruction here. But each time they were shortly suppressed. Even in their own houses, inhabitants of Boston are forbidden to engage in singing or dancing or fiddling. The town watchmen take note of offenders. No wonder the dauntless of heart travel out of our town, from tavern to tavern, and at a safe distance engage in drinking and revelry. Even the playing of football in the streets has been forbidden by the Town Meeting, ever since several bystanders received injuries during the youngsters' games. These strictures suffocate me quite as much as the gag of the Devil. *The place is too strait for me, give room that I may dwell,* says the Prophet.

I have been thinking about a further restriction: The law requires the consent of her parents before a girl may receive the attention of an admirer. I wonder if my mistress will insist on adhering to this rule. After all, I am not her daughter. But why should I trouble to wonder? There's no imminent danger of the question arising.

Negra says some masters deny their Negroes the

privilege of marriage altogether. They insist upon chastity for creatures of dark skin. The Negro babies are of so little value, they are sometimes disposed of like a litter of puppies. Indeed, it seems that Negroes are considered by us to be only half-human. A cow in our vicinity brought forth a calf that had so much of a human visage as to convince the inhabitants the poor animal had been impregnated by a Negro.

Would Redmen be drawn to so monstrous a conclusion?

I am not surprised to learn that not all of the English captives were eager to return to civilization. Having lived a while among the Indians, though ransomed by friend or family, some of our English became disgusted with our manner of life, and the care and pains necessary to support it, and took the first opportunity of escaping again into the woods. Despite the ministry of such good men as Mr. John Eliot, it is conceded that in all relations, peaceful and hostile, between Red men and White, the proportion of Whites barbarized to Indians civilized is as a hundred to one. Is it possible our resistance to the wilderness has not been strong enough? Our English must have missed, as I do, the life lived close to the earth and under an endless sky. Even women have been known to desert our ways in favor of the Redmen's.

I have already discussed these desertions with my mistress. She declares herself unable to judge of them, having never lived among the Red tribes.

"Are you sorry for that?" I ask her.

She laughs, calls me mischievous, and hands me a busy task.

When I spoke of the renegade English to Mr.

Mather, he cleared his throat and said these unfortunate souls have been abandoned into Satan's power. "Never forget," he thundered, "that these traitors have made their gain by trading pieces, powder and shot to the Indians. And then they have taught the Savages how to use 'em, to charge and discharge, and what proportion of powder to give the piece, according to the size of the same. And what shot to use for fowl and what for deer. And so the Savages have become far more active in that employment than any of the English, by reason of their swiftness of feet and nimbleness of body, being also quick-sighted and by continual exercise well knowing the haunts of all sorts of game. Thus the natives have become mad (as it were) after guns, accounting their bows and arrows but baubles in comparison to them. How many English have lately been slain by those Indians thus furnished! O that princes and parliaments would take some timely order to punish these gain-thirsty murderers, these traitors to their neighbors and their country! The blood of their brethren sold for gain!"

As on all such occasions when Mr. Mather becomes agitated by a remark or rumor I have introduced, he grows ever more inflamed. "Let us sing a mighty psalm!" he cries.

I sing at the top of my voice, with great good cheer. Mr. Mather's voice comes tumbling out like a cartwheel bumping on cobbles.

> *The vengeance falls on those*
> *Who follow evil ways;*
> *They vanish from our view:*
> *Their triumphs fade away.*

My mistress has told me that Mr. Mather was a mere youth at Harvard College when his speech impediment caused great anxiety lest he fail to follow in the distinguished footsteps of his minister father and grandfathers. Elijah Corley, one of Mr. Mather's old schoolmasters, was consulted. He advised the lad to speak with *dilated deliberation*. And since in singing the mouth is relieved of stammering, so by prolonging his pronunciation as in a slow psalm, Mr. Mather was assisted to acquire the habit of speaking without hesitation. Smooth discourse leaves him only when he is most agitated. I try not to alarm him. I try not to become alarmed myself when Mr. Mather reminds me that his congregation paid six pounds for my ransom. Nor when he urges me, one more time, to maintain my journal more responsibly. I should not, he repeats, put down whatever comes into my mind, but rather only those matters which bear upon Christian conduct and my rescue from the Devil.

Dec. 25

> Dark the Indian child is born,
> bright the noon toward which it grows.
> Dark the seed until the morn
> blooms it heavenward pink and rose.
> Gold the coming day, as corn.
>
> Darker, deeper far than I:
> infant in my English arm.
> Pray the Chiefs who rule the sky
> never let me come to harm,
> never let my infant die.

When Mr. Mather finally arrived here after his second sermon, I showed him the verses I had written, and sang them for him, to the tune of "The Ravished Maiden." I had expected praise for my composition. For I had spent the Lord's Day solitude in setting down my thoughts in rhyme. And I had picked a pleasing ballad rhythm to accompany the stanzas.

But Mr. Mather complained that the popular ballad was a rough one, and that I should not have used its tune. Furthermore, he did not understand my verses. He said he found nothing of spiritual song in their creation. I spoke up boldly in their defense and angered Mr. Mather with my argument.

He asked me what I meant by "the Chiefs who rule the sky." "There is only one Lord in Heaven," he roared.

I replied, spiritedly, that there are the Father, the Son, and the Holy Ghost, and *they* are the three divine Chiefs or sachems.

"Never blaspheme, child!"

I do not like to be addressed as *child.*

He continued very stern, saying that Satan must be working upon me through this rude ballad music.

I defied him to prove it was so. I had been quite at peace, I assured him, the whole day through. Searching and sifting rhymes had given me happy occupation, deep comfort.

"False occupation! False comfort!" he fairly screamed. His eyes blazed, and a fleck of spittle lurked in the corner of his mouth. He most resembled those crazy Tigers of Hell clothed in flames of fire, eyes flaring like the light of a lanthorn accommodated with a glass globe to increase the candle glow.

His anger so frightened me, I could make no response. How had I dared to defy him? I wanted to apologize, but could not. I recovered sufficiently to remind him that Mistress Anne Bradstreet had written a whole quantity of poems, and that some of them had even been published.

"Beware the boundless and sickly appetite for the reading of poems!" he shouted. "This rickety nation is swarming with that foolish craving. Study mortification, child! Heaven-sent mortification! Read Michael Wigglesworth! His are Godly verses!"

Will Mr. Mather be displeased that I have written

66

this account in my journal? Is the Devil at his tricks again? What hand is filling these pages? Mine, the true Mercy Short? Or the dread Bewitched one?

Abruptly the minister left me and went up the stairs to the room overhead. Then it was that I heard and felt most plainly and paganly a dance as of a barefoot man. And those attending me heard and felt the same, and would willingly take their oath on it. Is the Devil at his old tricks, mixing a poisonous brew for me again? Surely Evil must be following me all my days if I can no longer distinguish the Fiend from Mr. Mather himself?

My mistress was upset with my behavior and told me so, oh very strenuously. "It's a wonder," she concluded, "Mr. Mather did not chastise you for your insolence." She said the same to Mr. Mather when at length he came downstairs.

I made a demure face, and murmured:

I am thy patient pupil.

Under my breath I went on in Edward Taylor's *Meditation*:

Thou art my Priest, Physician, Prophet, King,
Lord, Brother, Bridegroom, Father, Everything.

But Mr. Mather disagreed with my mistress. "No, never. Corporal punishment is an abomination. My father and grandfathers held to that opinion before me. Oh I had my share of whippings from father and schoolmasters. But I also had goodly rewards of raisins and citron, and candy and sugared almonds, and cider, and warmed beer. I would never give a child a *blow*, except in case of obstinacy, or some gross

67

enormity. As a parent I try to practice a sweet authority and avoid such harshness and fierceness as may discourage my children. Our authority should be so tempered with kindness, and meekness, and loving tenderness, that our children may *fear* us with delight—"

I interrupted, asking him to explain, but he continued:

"—and see that we love them with as much delight. I reward my children with teaching them some curious thing, and punish them by withdrawing that reward. And I do not forget the spiritual and practical education of my young Maria."

But he lost little Abigail at barely five months. I have read his published sermon on her death. "Our children," he preached, "who were on loan are not lost, but given back." How difficult, how severe a belief. I cannot in my heart subscribe to it. I have sad cause to wonder at the truth of it.

Never, never have I experienced more unbelief than when my bastard infant died.

At this moment Mr. Mather advises me, as on many occasions, that I must take greater care in keeping my journal. "Confine your observations to the matters that deeply concern us. Avoid repeating idle gossip. Restrain yourself from joining forces with Devilish influences."

My thoughts are confused about those Devilish influences. I ask him to explain.

"Take care lest the Devil turn you against me."

The Devil turn me against Mr. Mather? Never!

"The Devil," he insists, "has been known to enter the hearts of men against me. Even the hearts of the Governor and the Council, when Mr. Bradstreet and the others suppressed our first and only newspaper."

My mistress nods vigorously in confirmation.

Mr. Mather acknowledges her silent testimony and continues, "Certainly I approve of the three purposes of *Public Occurrences*: to reveal memorable providences, to inform citizens of events in the public world, and to chastise the spirit of lying which prevails amongst us."

My mistress cannot contain herself. "Even more serious," she interposes, "have been the attempts to discredit the name of Mather with cursed reproaches from unworthy, ungodly, ungrateful persons."

But everyone knows that Mr. Mather is a man of the most fulgid endowments. His enlargements and attainments are everywhere held up for praise. He himself refers often to the scores of publications which have been surprised from his hand. And the macerating exercises of prayer and fasting he undertakes.

What kind of reproaches? I beg the good minister to share these abuses with me, so that I may compose prayers of my own against them.

Mr. Mather takes a deep breath. "I have been ridiculed for assuming the deliverance of yourself from the Devil. I have been criticized on the ground of ordering you to count me your father, and regard me and obey me. Some of our learned witlings of the coffeehouse have mocked my proofs of an Invisible World, turning them all into sport. I have been blamed for spending so much time with you, because of my interest in your condition; for attempting to rescue you from the Lions and Bears of Hell. I have been attacked by people of a peculiar dirtiness with sly, naked, unpretending insinuations that I have behaved indecorously with you. They say they have been witness, here in your bedchamber, to immodest behavior on my part, such as laying hands on your stomach and breast, though you protested against my meddling. Yet the oaths of the spectators can testify that it was upon the *pillow,* at a distance from your *body,* that the Imp was apprehended."

"Of course, on the *pillow,*" I agree.

But am I quite certain?

"You cannot but know how much these false representations have contributed to make people believe a smutty thing of me. Gossips say that on such occasions I have ordered the company of people to withdraw, the very company I invited to pray with you. One woman cried out that she was sure she was no Witch, and therefore would not go. So others; so none withdrew. Thus you see, my dear Mercy, I must pray harder than ever, and you with me, for your salvation. As the minister who invited you into Christian service, I have a sort of *right* to demand your deliverance from these invading Devils, and to demand such a *liberty* for you as might make you capable of glorifying my glorious Lord."

How little have I suspected the magnitude of Mr. Mather's suffering and shame on my behalf! It is now clear to me, it *must* be clear to me, I *owe* it to him to recover. If I did not, I should be disgracing him utterly. I have written down what I recall of his words, for my own reproach to myself, to be read over and over when I wander from true feelings of humility and gratitude.

To think that there have been times when I cried out that the Specter tormenting me appeared in the very guise of Mr. Mather! To think I have complained that it was Mr. Mather himself who threatened and molested me! How could I have believed such blasphemy, much less uttered it aloud? Fortunately, as soon as the fit passed I implored Mr. Mather to pray all the more passionately for me. No wonder he expressed dismay, increasingly every time, at my accusations. No wonder the company surrounding us drew noxious conclusions. No wonder he speaks of walking softly and sorrowfully as long as he breathes on earth.

It must have been the Devil, still unsubdued, who whispered hissing in my ear that the minister was nonetheless proud of the threat to his reputation.

Dec. 26

It has been decided by Dr. Oakes and Mr. Mather that I am not yet ready to return home to my mistress. Especially Mr. Mather wishes me to remain here, close to the meetinghouse. He will continue to look in on me as he comes and goes. I am still a case of Demonic possession; his work is not yet completed. His written account of my Bewitchment is of the utmost importance. He studies my journal to discover evidence beyond his own observations.

But I no longer enjoy putting down on paper the antics of the Fiends. I think it might be better now to forget them, or at least ignore them. They come out of hiding at the very moment I pick a quill. They hoot and dance with glee while I am recording their behavior. I am more at peace when I knit a pair of stockings for one of my sisters, or stir the porridge heating on the hearth. My appetite begins to revive with the good fumes.

My mistress has asked me to sharpen her sewing needles. I enjoy poking them in and out of her little emery bag, a bright red strawberry shape. I pretend it's the Imp himself I am penetrating, and quite enjoy the task.

I wish I had a piece of strawberry bread, as the Indians prepared it, the berries bruised in a mortar and mixed with meal. Strawberries are still my favorite fruit, though sometimes we had no other food for many days. We were glad for the abundance of the little red cones. Did God ever make a better berry?

Thanks to my improving appetite, I am scarcely an invalid any longer. As soon as the weather moderates I shall gain strength enough to send the Specters packing for the last time. We are all shut in, imprisoned together in this fine house. I long for the sky above me. How wide it stretched over us in our captivity!

I feel like those solitary, shiny black-bodied salamanders that tunnel underground in spring, to remain for more than eleven months of the year. But in March, when the early rains begin, a change takes place. I have seen the creatures climb to the surface and crawl through the leaf litter to the nearest small kettle hole. We had to push through thick tangles of briar, highbush blueberry and other shrubs to approach the little pockets of runoff which are the salamanders' destination. Early on the march we watched their progress by dusk toward the annual mating ritual. It lasted only a few nights before they disappeared underground for the better part of a year again. How strange was their sinuous courtship in a group, under pond water still glazed with skim ice. Before the small short-lived breeding places evaporate to a moist patch of leaves and mud, the once-a-year adventurers have long since raced back to their underground existence. By August even the newly developed young salamanders join the life of darkness.

Must I suffer eleven months of darkness?

There is a youth in the men's chorus whose voice is sweeter than the others. I listen for him as I might look for an orchis among commoner plants, the fragrant purple-fringed orchis. His echo lingers tenderly in my ears while I read a favorite book.

Despite Mr. Mather's outburst against poems, my mistress lets me keep her copy of Anne Bradstreet's collection, to pass the time. She doubts the verses will do me harm.

My dumpish thoughts, my groans, my brackish tears,
My sobs, my longing hopes, my doubting fears . . .
Tell him I would say more but cannot well.

Even Mistress Bradstreet had her sinkings and droopings. Shall I not have mine? And shall I not sometime savor, as she did taste, of the hidden manna that my world yet knows not?

Dec. 27

A late December thaw.

I slipped out of the house this morning and stumbled, shaky invalid that I am, along the wharves. How closely and confidently the paths and lanes of Boston follow the scalloped sea-front! The sight of shops and shipping, ocean and scattered islands, the dense wooded islands of the harbor, was a tonic to my eyes. Vessels of all shapes and sizes: shallops, sloops, hoys, pinnaces; bark, brig, ketch and lighter. And the busy lumbering dance of mechanical cranes, loading and unloading cargoes. Impossible, though I tried, to count the artisans and laborers who care for the ships riding in the Bay, the carpenters, smiths, caulkers, braziers. While the men called out cheerfully to me, I stepped with caution beside the rope walks, and peered into sailmakers' lofts. I filled my lungs with the keen smells assailing my nostrils: pungence of new wood issuing from the carpenters' shops, the half-unpleasant odor of the tanning pits, fiery metalic whiffs from the blacksmith's forge, and always the sea, the sea!

A wild desire seized me to sail away on one of the great, handsome creatures frozen unmoving, or gently swaying where the ice in the harbor had begun to melt—*wooden birds,* Sam Danforth calls them in his Almanac verse. Or I'd wait for one of those ketches soon to return from winter voyaging in the West Indies, relieved of their Boston cargo of salt cod and mackerel, barrels of flour, salt beef, firkins of butter. They'd come laden with logwood, indigo, cocoa, sugar, pieces of eight and bullion. Yes, and then I'd sail in early spring, laden partly with Caribbean products, partly with beaver by the hogshead and truss, and moose skins by the hundred. I'd cross the great Atlantic like a seabird, to land in London and exchange cargoes with the English. And maybe save some of our fish cargo for Spain and the Wine Isles, in order to bring back salt from Cadiz, iron from Bilboa, wine from Xeres and the Western Islands.

Dear compassionate God, am I never in this life to make a voyage, not even such as the least Negro on being imported for sale? Is the captive march to Quebec, the confused sea journey back, to remain the single adventure of my life? Grant me an adventure in freedom, dear Lord! Even only to Virginia for tobacco, even only that!

What is the meaning of my restlessness of soul? I find in myself an adverse spirit, a trembling heart. I am less willing to submit to the will of God than the Scripture requires of me. Yes, for some time now I have been loath to enter into strict bonds with the Lord.

I stood on the edge of the dock and cried aloud the fourteenth verse of REVELATION 12: *And to the woman were given two wings of a great eagle, that she might fly into the wilderness, into her place, where she is nourished. . . .*

I turned from the sea. Out of the King's Head Tavern, near Scarlett's Wharf, I caught the whiff of burnt Madeira and plum cake. I thought I heard a familiar voice singing "The Lovesick Maiden." I felt faint and about to fall. Someone helped me back to the house.

I was not surprised to be roundly scolded. But I *was* surprised—and disturbed—to discover myself *invoking* my ghostly Tormentor. Is it not curious, I now seem to experience the Devilry at will, as though I am myself the originator of these distinct and formal fits of Bewitchment?

Mr. Mather declares such invention impossible. "You are no Witch, foolish Mercy. You cannot *devise* your seizures from within you. There is truly a Devil, as there is truly a God. And both are *outside* you."

I have lost interest in this journal. I am keeping it only to please Mr. Mather. I hardly remember the moments of possession—for they are now merely moments, of no duration—clearly enough to write them down.

What if I should ignore them completely?

Dec. 28

The nine o'clock bell is already striking from the meetinghouse, and I have written down not so much as a word in my journal the whole long day.

Neighborhood women are praying with us. They put me in mind of quilting parties back in Salmon Falls. How safe and peaceful I felt among the women, my mother among them, not a man, not even my father, attending.

What is it about a man that inspires excitement, even fear?

How industriously the women worked their fingers! I brought them food and drink, and listened to the lively gossip of country matters, the crops, the latest brush with Indians, a new baby. Someone would tell of the recent arrival of fabrics imported from London or Bristol. News from Boston always delighted us. The women kept working as long as there was light to work by. The thread on the spinning wheel in the corner was tested and praised. All of us, goodwife and child, could distinguish the quality of linen and wool. At my mother's bidding I recited, more than willingly, Edward Taylor's "Housewifery."

78

> Make me, O Lord, Thy spinning-wheel complete;
> Thy holy words my distaff make for me.
> Make mine affections Thy swift flyers neat,
> And make my soul Thy holy spool to be,
> My conversation make to be Thy reel,
> And reel the yarn thereon spun of Thy wheel.
> Make me Thy loom then, knit therein this twine:
> And make Thy Holy Spirit, Lord, wind quills:
> Then weave the web Thyself. The yarn is fine.

and so on and so on, very expressively, with eyes uplifted soulfully to the ceiling. How many poems learned, how many stockings, mittens, tippets knitted in my short life!

According to Mr. Mather, I should be scrupulously candid in my journal-keeping. I should not neglect to mention my vanity, an immodest pride in my memory, especially for recalling poems. I always hoped one of our country neighbors would remember to ask for my favorite Taylor verses, "The Preface." Without the least hesitation I would launch into the lines, barely waiting for the request. I was thundering like a prophet of old by the time I came to

> Who blew the bellows of His furnace vast?
> Or held the mould wherein the world was cast?
> Who laid in corner stone? Or whose commands?
> Where stand the pillars upon which it stands?
> Who lac'd and filleted the earth so fine,
> With rivers like green ribbons smaragdine?
> Who made the sea's its selvedge, and its locks
> Like a quilt ball within a silver box?
> Who spread its canopy? Or curtains spun?
> Who in this bowling alley bowled the sun?
> Who made it when it rises always set:
> To go at once both down, and up to get?

Oh I do love the roaring sound of religion as the poet records it! The voice of faith is a splendid booming, blasting, awe-filled throat, more terrible even than the Devil's!

Women's gatherings, women's talk, how comforting. How blest and glad I am to be safe again in a woman's care, in the service of my widowed mistress. What if I *am* fatherless now? What if the Devil tells me so, over and over again mocking me? I reply I have God for a father. And of course Mr. Mather.

In Salmon Falls I had both mother and father, beloved both. I pleaded with them, that last autumn, insisting I was already old enough to attend the corn husking. And at length they consented. Oh the Devilish red ear! How excited the fellow who found it! How enflamed we grew on kisses and drams! Songs were sung, but not of the psalm kind. Youth and maid were locked in each other's arms, as though jesting, yet not jesting. Sometimes a pair left the barn and were gone long enough to raise a question among us. By early spring there were young girls in need of a wedding. There was more than one farmer's daughter who had secretly shelled red corn at planting season into her father's seed basket. We helped our chances.

Months later, when I watched the Indians celebrating in their frenzied fashion, I was at once reminded of our country custom. I could not resist joining in with tribesmen and squaws. Our merrymaking disguised the melancholy of my memories, as with strong drink. When I wrestled with the handsome sannup it was scarcely different from our jostling and tumbling against one another in the New Hampshire barn. I discovered how I might be briefly, strangely, happy, even in the wilderness.

Dec. 29

Early awake, before the five o'clock meetinghouse bell. I have been reading the gloomy verses of Michael Wigglesworth, as Mr. Mather directs me. I have no heart for them, they are such somber, dusty, prosy stuff. There is no juice in 'em.

Now my mistress has arrived, to my great relief, brightening the gloom. She brings a hasty pudding and news of the town. A dyer has lately come from England and set up business in Boston. He can dye all sorts of colors, she says, after the best manner and cheapest rate. Scarlets, crimsons, pinks, purples, straws, wine colors, sea greens. And Mr. Hull has a new shipload from England: mainly textiles, and most welcome at this inclement time of year. Bales of dowlas, duffel, cambric and say; bright-colored penistones, sad-colored serges and kerseys. Oh how I long to feel the delicious stuffs in my fingers! A shipment of little coral whistles is now to be found in the shops. I must buy one for my young sister.

The Devil has lately shown me very splendid garments, which he promises to give me if I but sign his book. How I long for a new gown in a brilliant shade! I think I should feel quite cured and lively in it. When

I express my heart's craving, my mistress laughs and quotes Edward Taylor:

Dost Thou adorn some thus, and why not me?

But it's true, these clothes are drab and stinking. I am grateful my mistress lights a spermaceti candle as dusk comes on. I ask her to snuff it for a moment. The sweetness of its scent when the flame is extinguished floods the room, and enters the layers of my garments. How soft and easy, when re-lighted, its expanding glow. It is like balm to my sorely Bedevilled eyes, bringing the object close to my sight, rather than causing the eyes to trace half blindly after it, as all tallow candles do, from a certain dimness which they produce.

I like this fragrance better than the pungent bayberry. Last month we converted three bushels of bayberry into almost four pounds of wax. Adding the same amount of mutton fat, we made some fine taperware. Best of all I like the bayberries wrapped in muslin and rubbed on the iron, to freshen the laundry being pressed.

Dec. 30

The crier of fish has passed by the door. I have a sudden, ravenous appetite.

I opened the stillroom door, and only sharpened my pangs of hunger. Oh the dizzying smells of cheeses, wines and beers! And the colorful preserves all lined up in a delectable rainbow: damsons, quinces, pears, plums, cherries, barberries, apples, raspberries. I closed the door quickly, before I should be tempted to steal a morsel or a dram.

My mistress arrives at last with a savory pork dish, and news of an excommunication at the Mather church. The highest censure will be passed, next Lord's Day, upon a young woman of the congregation, for her crime of adultery. I should like to look at the face of an adulteress. I need to examine her bearing. *For the woman which hath an husband is bound by the law to her husband so long as he liveth. . . . So then if, while her husband liveth, she be married to another man, she shall be called an adulteress.* ROMANS 7:2–3.

Mr. Mather says we should always refer public events to our own condition.

But I was a maiden still in the wilderness.

How shall a virgin determine the vileness of her sin?

Mr. Mather assures me his own heart contains inclinations which would make him as vile as the vilest, but for the sovereign grace of God.

I have looked deep into a mirror for the first time in many days. My face is the countenance of a stranger. I am lean and drawn from the long fasting. My eyes are sunken and haunted. My hair has lost its gold light. What a miserable aspect I present! I must take comfort in the first book of CORINTHIANS 1:27–28. *But God hath chosen the foolish things of the world to confound the wise; and God hath chosen the weak things of the world to confound the things which are mighty; And base things of the world, and things which are despised, hath God chosen. . . .*

Yes, it is a foolish, weak, despised thing which confronts me in the mirror. My soul is shriveled. My lips are dry and cracked. But oh my dear Lord, my mouth is watering! A drunken fragrance is filling the room. Oh bless this food! The stewed pork is delicious. We kept pigs in Salmon Falls. I loved to watch the Pig Run, a favorite contest among our youth. My brother Richard took the prize, one year, for seizing the greased pig and fairly holding it by the tail. Where are you now, Richard? I grant the Pig Run is a cruel sport. But we found it vastly entertaining, nonetheless. Do I see a Black Pig lumbering toward me from the hearth? Quick! I'll rush toward it as though to kick it! Good! It has vanished. The Specters vanish if I can but run toward 'em. A useful ruse to intimidate 'em.

Mr. Mather comes by with his wife, who was Abigail Phillips of Charlestown. She was not yet sixteen at the time of their marriage. In that very week of May, an unmarried servant in her father's house gave unexpected birth. What was her punishment, I wonder? No one can tell me whether the baby still survives. The Mathers' own firstborn died barely a year later. My mistress heard the bereaved father deliver the funeral sermon. Auditors were struck by the depth and dignity of his grief. How did the bereft mother, poor Mrs. Mather, contain her sorrow? I have no right to speak to her of her loss. She would suffer at the reminder. Have I courage to tell her of my own misfortune, to compare our griefs? Why do I return continually to morbid questioning? According to Negra, Mr. Mather's father's maid was brought to bed of a child out of wedlock. Her master turned her out of the house. These are iron times we live in.

Mrs. Mather apologizes for their haste in departing. She tells us that Mr. Mather is a wonderful improver of time. He has a sign over his study door: BE SHORT. His sermons are not short, to that I can attest. Many's the Sabbath I have nibbled at herbs, dill or fennel or sprigs of caraway which my mistress brought along to meeting, in order to keep me from drowsing.

My mistress recalls particular occasions when pirates and other criminals were taken to the meeting-house in chains and forced to listen to a sermon concerning their sins, before a crowded congregation. She remembers all too vividly a fast-day service some years before I was brought to Boston. "In the first place," she recounts, "a minister read a prayer in the pulpit of full two hours' duration; after which an old minister delivered a sermon an hour long, and after that a prayer was made and some verses sung out of a psalm. In the afternoon three or four hours were consumed with nothing except prayers, three ministers relieving each other alternately. When one was tired, another went up into the pulpit."

Oh my poor mistress! Much good the hourglass on the pulpit did her!

And oh, poor me, Mercy Short, when a psalm tune has well over one hundred lines! Still worse, we girls and women may not even join in the singing, not in the meetinghouse, only in our own sequestered praying companies. Imagine our boredom and distress, tight-lipped as we must remain, while we listen to the most drawling, quavering discord in the world! The deacon sets the tune, very often in noticeable uncertainty, then lines out the psalm, verse by verse, while the male congregation follows, so to speak, his lead. Now indeed it's every man for himself, with little regard for what his bombastic neighbors might be doing. Added to this Pandemonium, the boys often smuggle their dogs into the meeting, and the tithing man has to climb righteously up the ladder to the gallery, where the poor and the slaves take their greatest satisfaction in egging on the furor.

But my mistress reminds me that Mr. Mather is among those concerned to improve the congregational singing. I am glad to hear it.

As for *being short*, Mr. Mather's visits have lately become short indeed. He used to spend many hours comforting me. All the same, he never took me into his house, as he did the Bewitched Martha Goodwin. Six months or more she remained close by him. What was young Mrs. Mather meanwhile thinking of the Bedevilled thirteen-year-old, flying about the room like a goose or riding all over the house, even upstairs and down, on an invisible horse? It shied, the possessed girl claimed, at Mr. Mather's door. I don't doubt it: She wanted to go *in*! I understand the saucy girl. One can read the account in the words of the good minister himself. He even went so far as to admit her into his private study. Was he well advised? Did he remember to *be short* with her? In his room, not surprisingly, she felt at ease. As who should not. She continued, to be sure, to engage in fits so dangerous Mr. Mather had to use physical force to contain her. I should like to have seen *that*!

Here is one episode of the affair, in Mr. Mather's published record. I find it worth copying.

It gave me much trouble to get her into my arms, and much more to drag her up the stairs. She was pulled out of my hands, and when I recovered my hold, she was thrust so hard upon me, that I had almost fallen backwards, by the Devils' compressions to detain her. With incredible forcing (though she kept screaming, "They say I must not go in!") at length we pulled her in: where she was no sooner come, but she could stand on her feet, and with an altered tone, could thank me, saying, "Now I am well."

And what was Mrs. Mather thinking all this while? Did she too have tender patience with the frenzied Martha? I should think not. They say Mrs. Mather neglected to smother a laugh when Martha rode her unseen hobbyhorse up and down the stairs and all around the house. Whereupon, only shortly thereafter, the Devil himself appeared to the minister's wife on her own porch, so frightening her that she gave premature birth to a deformed and short-lived baby. Is no one, not even the minister's wife, safe from the Devil?

Here's a passage begs to be copied down:

She would knock at my study door, affirming that someone below would be glad to see me, yet there was none that had asked for me. She would call to me with multiplied impertinencies, and throw small things at me wherewith she could not give me any hurt. She'd hector me at a strange rate for the work I was at, and threaten me with I know not what mischief for it.

Well, why did he let her carry on without hindrance?

She had gotten a history that I had written of this Witchcraft, and though she had before this read it over and over, yet now she could not read (I believe) one sentence of it, but she made of it the most ridiculous travesty in the world, with such a patness and excess of fancy, to supply the sense that she put upon it, as I was amazed at. And she particularly told me, that I would quickly come to disgrace by that history.

Poor patient Mr. Mather!

Martha's Bedevilment, in appearance so resembling my own, quite seizes my interest. How should I have behaved, I wonder, had Mr. Mather taken me into his house? More reasonable than the Goodwin creature, of this I am certain. Why did he not take me in? Did Mrs. Mather dissuade him? It is a matter well known here, that he offered to take half a dozen of the Bewitched Salem girls into his personal care, under his very roof. I rejoice for Mrs. Mather that they remained in Salem.

But what about my own recovery? Would it not have proceeded more congenially in the minster's closer care? Was he as cherishing a father as might have been? Why did he see fit to deprive me of his most intimate supervision? Surely he did not doubt the gravity of my symptoms? Did he think I might be *inventing* wild behavior and conversation, after the irresponsible manner of Martha Goodwin? But my Fiends are authentic, this he must know for a fact. On the contrary, Martha's ravings have a false ring to them. Surely I am equipped to judge them.

Well, Devil, what do you say? How many more fits am I to have? Pray, can you tell me how long it shall be before you are hanged for what you have done? No, you are filthy Witches. You would have killed me, but you can't. I don't fear you. You would have thrown Mr. Mather downstairs, but you could not. Hark you, one thing more before we part: What hurt is it you will do to Mrs. Mather? Will you do her any hurt? Oh, I am glad of it, they can do Mrs. Mather no hurt. They try, but they say they can't.

Anyone can tell these are the ravings of a child permitted to have her sport with an adult. Why did Mr. Mather allow the girl to disgrace him with her lies and jokings? Or did he, after all, enjoy these irregular encounters? *Ingenious child,* he writes. *She became charmed with my person to such a degree that she could not but break in upon me with her most importunate requests.*

Does this Godly man then believe I too am charmed with his person?

What a patient woman must Mrs. Mather be! How fortunate that the authorities in Salem did not accept her husband's excessive offer. Well, at least one Mercy Short is not straining Mrs. Mather's indulgence under her roof. My own mistress grows lately impatient, and properly so. And the hospitable family which has taken me into their dwelling, they must be hoping for my prompt recovery and return home. Yet not more urgently than I myself am hoping. I *must* recover, and quickly. If only to rid myself of these *Day of Doom* verses Mr. Mather keeps pressing upon me, for my salvation.

> *They say, they roar, for anguish sore,*
> *And gnaw their tongues for horror.*

What a foul couplet! The stench of the lines fairly sickens me.

Someone calls attention to a strong odor hovering about the house. A cheese has been removed from the stillroom press. Afterwards it is found right here upon the table, hidden under my apron. God is a great forgiver.

Dec. 31

The year ends in great happiness. My mistress has brought me a new gown, not exceptionally vivid in coloring, of a common blue, but fresh and signifying the cheer and proportion my life shall henceforth attain. I throw my arms about her, quoting the line from Edward Taylor:

I leap for joy to think, shall these be mine?

She laughs to show that she is not seriously admonishing me, though she remarks that I use the versified Scripture for my irreligious delight. I might have preferred a golden tissue dyed the singing color of yellow broom, proof against sad or sober thoughts. They call the plant Witches' Blood in Salem, where it grows on Gallows Hill.

I dressed myself and called for Mr. Mather, to show him how splendid I looked. I am still extremely weak and sickly. But I faced Mr. Mather with a suitable look of discretion and gravity, and told him my invincible Tormentors had left, just before, in very raging terms, and that they had no further power over me.

"Now go," I enjoined Mr. Mather, "and give the great God the greatest thanks you can devise, for I am gloriously delivered!" We sang a hymn together, just Mr. Mather and I.

> *Today the reign of Satan ends,*
> *His Kingdom's overthrown.*

Neighbors joined us in thanks that I had at last been given *to tread upon the lion and adder: the young lion and the dragon shalt thou trample under feet.* PSALM 91:13

Mr. Mather has calculated that the reign of anti-Christ will end, according to the Book of Revelation, in the year 1697. Is not my deliverance a shining signal of the approaching Millennium, in that God has clogged my Adversaries? Let God but continue to clog them, and all will be well. "All the peace of New England," says Mr. Mather, "lies in her being *a wise virgin,* that shall go forth to meet the marvelous effusion of God's spirit upon the nations."

Before leaving for home with my mistress, I learned the name of the youth with the fine voice—Joseph Marshall.

Joseph Marshall.

This is the end of my journal.

1693

Feb. 19

After six weeks blessedly free of the Demons, here I am again helpless in their power.

Mr. Mather has come a distance to my mistress's house to examine me. He reminds me, without delay, to write down my thoughts and fits and seizures in a journal. He brings more sheets of paper, a thick packet of them. He cannot visit me so long or so often as in December, those anxious weeks when I was invalided close by the meetinghouse. Once again I have been taken captive by the Specters on the Lord's Day during Mr. Mather's sermon. He was preaching about Pray for Life, But Prepare for Death. The solemn thrust of his text was a knife into my Sabbath yearnings. Some auditors declared themselves hardly able to forbear crying out aloud during the sermon. How shall I hope to thrive amid all this joylessness?

"Shame be my garment, grief my meat, tears my drink, and sighs my language," thunders Mr. Mather, "as long as I am related to this *vile body*!"

How shall I not despair of surviving such heartless expectations?

"Lord, I here take my vow, that I will never give

95

Thee, or my own soul rest, until my dearest lusts become as bitter as death, as hateful as Hell unto me."

Dear God, I have already witnessed death so close at hand, so many deaths, great deaths even, and that one sweet small flame extinguished. I cannot now bear to consider my own death. I will pray, pray, pray for *Life*!

A cry of *Fire!* was made, which much disturbed us in the midst of the sermon. It proved to be Recompense Moody's chimney, which occasioned a great light. Snow on the housetops prevented danger.

The past Lord's Day completed the thirtieth year of Mr. Mather's life. The congregation surrounded him after the service, to bless him with their good wishes. Envious Fiends took the strength out of my legs and kept me from approaching him. He was forced to brush aside the crowd and come to see me on my mistress's bench where I lay stricken with terror. My good mistress has always kept me close beside her at the meeting, rather than send me to the balcony with the other indentured girls.

Dr. Oakes diagnosed an hysteric fit, and called for a chamber pot. My nose was bleeding profusely. Someone quickly fetched a dried toad from the apothecary and hung it about my neck. The bleeding abated, but not the rigor of my limbs. A touch of Mr. Mather's hand restored me sufficiently so that I could be helped out of the meetinghouse and driven home in a borrowed calash.

On my arrival, Dr. Oakes examined me thoroughly. Praise God I have not developed a wen anywhere on my body, else the learned doctor might recommend that a dead hand be laid upon it till the mortal damp strike sensibly into my flesh. Sometimes several repetitions of the treatment may be called for.

At the earliest possible moment Mr. Mather joined us. He was thoroughly gratified with the success of his preaching. Though the Fiends had hoped to mortify him with their raving presences, the good minister told us he remained unaffected and rightfully vindicated by the Lord's blessing upon him. "This morning," he went on, "I laid my sinful mouth in the dust on my study-floor. And I obtained fresh and sweet assurance from Him that although I have been the most loathsome creature in the world, yet His Holy Spirit shall with Sovereign Grace take possession of me, and employ my sinful mouth to become this day the trumpet of His glory. And the hearts of the inhabitants of the town have been strangely moved by what I have delivered among them."

I asked Mr. Mather if the Devils might be exercising their vengeance upon *my* poor body. He dismissed the suggestion.

Once again I must starve myself because the Fiend demands it. For a week I have eaten not so much as a spoonful of porridge, until this very morning. I have not had strength enough to write down my troubled thoughts until today, one whole week later than the onset. Mr. Mather zealously upbraids me. I know it is important for him to have an accurate account of what Satan is plotting upon me. He must deal with the Devil point by point. It is serious litigation. I try to recount everything I remember. I tell him this and that and the other, but Mr. Mather lays great store on the *written* record, elaborated in great detail. He is himself a tireless writer, and already a much published author.

97

Now it is the Lord's Day again, and I am alone except for Negra. I begged my mistress to let her stay. Negra sighs that she does not understand the sermon. But she likes to listen to the psalm singing. Mr. Mather has warned her of Divine displeasure if she does not fit herself for joining a church. "A man whom I had warned of similar failure," he advises her, "fell off a roof and received a blow, whereof he lay for some while as dead. But coming to himself, one of the first things he thought on was what I had said to him; under the sense whereof he quickly went and joined himself unto the church."

Negra sits close by me, humming contentedly and carving a little wooden poppet. Though she should not be whittling on the Sabbath, nevertheless I do not find it in my heart to restrain her.

The weather is as bitter as my spirit. It must be a record low temperature for mid-February. I had intended to use the Sabbath profitably by writing down my latest dialogue with the Devil. But the chill air numbs and blurs my memory of recent encounters. Though a good fire has been set in this room, the juices forced out at the ends of short kindling by the heat of the flame keep freezing into ice. On such a day as this the harbor quite hardens up. The Sacramental Bread will doubtless be frozen stiff, and rattle sorely as it is broken into the plates.

Before leaving for the meetinghouse, my mistress brought me hot cider and bade me give up this difficult effort of recall. "Mr. Mather himself once gave up a day of fasting during a similar cold spell. He saw it was impossible to serve the Lord while suffering such inconvenient distraction." She points out the passage in one of his pamphlets.

The cider warmed me not at all. Even though I sit

close to the hearth, I am chilled to the marrow, yet haunted by tremors of universal fires. What is this contradiction that besets me? I feel like that poor West Indian bird my mistress received as a gift. This country is too arctic for the frail creatures. The gilded cage hangs empty in the stillroom. You would think I had been born like Negra and the bird in Barbados, and not in New Hampshire, where the winters are even fiercer than here by the moderating Massachusetts Bay.

I remember a snowfall so violent it made all communication among our country neighbors impossible. Religious assemblies were cancelled throughout the region. Vast numbers of cattle were destroyed by the calamity. Some, of the strongest sort, were found standing dead on their legs, as if alive, many weeks after when the snow melted away. Their eyes were glazed over.

Many sheep were lost, my father's among them. Yet two creatures in a neighbor's flock were said to have survived in a singular manner. A month after the storm, when people were pulling out the ruins of over a hundred sheep buried in a sixteen-foot snowbank, they found two sheep alive. It was explained that they had kept themselves from expiring by eating the wool of their dead companions. I did not see this with my own eyes.

Alas for the deceits of winter! Our men of Salmon Falls dreamt that while the deep snow of March continued, they were safe enough from Indian attacks.

> Still was the night, serene and bright,
>   When all men sleeping lay;
> Calm was the season, and carnal reason
>   Thought it would last for aye.

99

But it was on that wintry dawn, nearly three years ago, that the French with the Indians, half one, half the other, half Indianized French, and half Frenchified Indians, fell suddenly upon our community. Oh my poor father, so viciously cut down, but not before seeing his wife ravaged and scalped and left to die!

> *For at midnight broke forth a light,*
> *Which turned the night to day,*
> *And speedily a hideous cry*
> *Did all the world dismay.*

Did Mr. Wigglesworth, with these gloomy doom-saying verses, mean our own poor innocent village in particular?

How my father must have suffered, as he lay dying, for the fate of his wife and children. For he had carried a burden of guilt with him all his New Hampshire years. Often I heard him question whether he should ever have left the town of Boston, its public worship and ordinances of God, to go live in a remote place, without the celebrated ministry of the Mathers, depriving, he said, "our selves and our children of so great benefit for our souls; and all this for worldly advantages."

> *So at midnight broke forth a light*
> *which turned the night to day,*

and did indeed change the course of my life, beyond hope of redemption. Mr. Mather says that Michael Wigglesworth's stanzas will continue to be read until the Day of Doom bids readers put it aside for the awful task of settling accounts with the Lord. I wish I did not dislike these somber verses so heartily. Our

Boston is verily a gloom-ridden town. I can well believe the story they tell of Captain Kemble who was set in the stocks for two hours on account of his lewd and unseemly behavior, which consisted of kissing his wife publicly on the Sabbath, on the doorstep of his house, just after he had returned from a three years' voyage.

Oh my dear good father, I miss you, miss you! I would not exchange those happy years in Salmon Falls for all the stocks and sermons in Boston!

Even our bitterest New Hampshire weather afforded us excitement. I remember tales of hogs and poultry surviving for three or four weeks under the snow. Deer and foxes came out of the woods. Great flocks of sparrows suddenly appeared, suddenly vanished. Orchards were severely damaged as animals walking on the crusted snow twelve feet above ground ate the tops and upper branches of the trees. And many boughs were split by the weight of ice and snow. Negra says that here in Boston she has seen the ocean in a prodigious winter ferment. After the storm, vast heaps of shells were driven ashore where they had not been seen before. And mighty shoals of porpoises played and frolicked in the troubled waters of the harbor. I should like to have seen that spectacle: porpoises playing their games in the midst of the Lord's anger!

Mr. Mather often reminds me that he is not interested in reading accounts of our happy family life in New Hampshire before the massacre. ''Do not dwell,'' he repeats, ''on the contented hours of your childhood. It is the Devil, only the Devil, we are concerned with here. We must confront him directly, from moment to moment, without deviation. We must not let him gain the advantage over us.''

Very well, the massacre, the captivity. And the march. Must I keep torturing myself with these memories? Well then, we were pinioned and led away that fateful dawn, over the hills in dark and hideous ways many miles farther before we took up our place for rest, which was in a dismal corner of the woods. We were kept bound all that first night. The Indians kept waking, and we ourselves had little mind to sleep. Our captors dispersed and, as they went, made strange noises as of wolves and owls and other wild beasts, to the end that they might not lose one another, and if followed they might not be discovered by the English.

A grim enough account?

Above all, I have been warned not to hanker after my young years, not to think of them as an innocent, Christian time of my life. *Suspect thyself much,* writes Thomas Shepard. Mr. Mather has pronounced the three awful words with special deliberation.

I have reread the psalm text of Mr. Mather's birthday sermon. *I said, O my God, take me not away in the midst of my days.* PSALM 102:24

If Mr. Mather feels thus sorely afflicted, how much more so do I!

My heart is smitten, and withered like grass; so that I forget to eat my bread. PSALM 102:4

Is the Lord strong enough to save me? If not, why do I continue struggling in His name?

The children of Thy servants shall continue, and their seed shall be established before Thee. PSALM 102:28

Shall my seed be indeed established? It has already once withered and perished. Shall it be established so that it endures? Where is the husband who is fated to make me again fruitful in my season? I despair of his finding me, cooped up as I am in this haunted chamber. I am too weak to go forth and search him out for myself. While I linger in the throes of Bewitchment I dare not venture into the streets of Boston, in the prayerful hope that I may find my destiny, and that I may be found by it. Marriage and hanging, they say, come by destiny.

I have pressed Mr. Mather, more than once, to tell me about my future. But he replies that today is the only day we are sure of. "Lose this NOW, and you shall never have another."

Negra puts her dark arms around me and comforts me with stories of her island home.

Feb. 26

Last Sunday after the morning service, Mr. Mather accompanied my mistress home. Negra was sent about her duties. I was cautioned against listening to her island reminiscences.

"But the Devil leaves me alone," I protest, "when I am listening to her."

"Idle amusement," says Mr. Mather, "is no substitute for prayer. Diversionary tactics will not keep the Devil at bay for long. Solid engagement with the problem of good and evil is your only hope. I am disappointed that you do not write daily in your journal. Persevere in your application! As often as you neglect to persevere, the Devil gains a point against you. One can hear the Fiend crying in Satanic glee whenever his sword finds a naked point of entry."

Is my life, then, to be one everlasting round of engagements against the Devil? Well, not even everlasting, not for this poor miserable span of my lifetime on earth. I must take some small grim comfort in the certainty that I have not long to suffer in this wretched body. But I am sick unto death of the skirmishing and scoring. How shall I ever escape that mortal combat, save with my death?

Once again, I have missed writing in my journal the whole week long. Today, the Lord's Day, I rally to the task. Mr. Mather has left with me a dread-inspiring quotation from Thomas Shepard. He urges me to commit it to memory so that I may keep it always in mind as a protection against wrong thinking. I am to recite it to him when I have it perfectly by heart. I have taken pride, since early childhood, in being an accomplished remembrancer. But these dire revilements thicken my tongue so that I cannot utter them. Let me test myself by writing them out. *Every natural man and woman is born full of all sin, as full as a toad is of poison, as full as ever his skin can hold; mind, will, eyes, mouth, every limb of his body, and every piece of his soul, is full of sin.*

No, dear Lord! Beloved, compassionate Lord! Do not let me believe such calumny! I have been a sinner, yes. And yet I cannot have sinned as greatly as some. Mistress Hutchinson, they say, guilty of thirty monstrous heresies, was delivered of as many monstrous births at once, every one of them greatly confused and altogether without form, small as an Indian bean or large as two male fists. And a woman infected with Anne Hutchinson's heresies gave birth to as hideous a monster as perhaps the sun ever looked upon. My mistress had marked the passage in Mr. Mather's book. *It had no head; the face was below the breast; the ears were like an ape's, and grew upon the shoulders; the eyes and mouth stood far out; the nose was hooking upwards; the breast and back were full of short prickles, like a thorn-back; the navel, belly, and the distinction of sex, which was female, were in the place of the hips; and those back parts were on the same side with the face; the arms, hands, thighs, and legs were as other children's; but instead of toes, it had on each foot three claws, with talons like a fowl; upon the back above the belly it had a couple of great holes like mouths; and in each of these stood out a couple of pieces of flesh; it had no forehead, but above the eyes it had four horns; two more than an inch long, hard and sharp; and the other two somewhat less.*

How dread are the punishings of the Lord! Why do I copy them down in their hideous details? Mr. Mather should spare me this anguish. He should counsel me against monstrous thoughts. I must ask him about the sins of the mothers being visited upon the infants.

Dear God, praise God, in Your great tenderness You loved my half-Indian baby. Yes, granted that I, Mercy Short, have sinned. But not the sinner's baby. The sinner's baby was a perfect little child of God. I have indeed committed an abomination. I do not deny it. I confess it over and over, reciting fervently the dark stanzas of Edward Taylor.

> *Still I complain; I am complaining still.*
> *O woe is me! Was ever heart like mine?*
> *A sty of filth, a trough of washing-swill,*
> *A dunghill pit, a puddle of mere slime,*
> *A nest of vipers, hive of hornet-stings,*
> *A bag of poison, civit-bag of sins.*

> *Was ever heart like mine? So bad? black? vile?*
> *Is any Devil blacker? Or can Hell*
> *Produce its match? It is the very soil*
> *Where Satan reads his charms and sets his spell.*

It is true, dear divine Punisher, I have sinned. But not my beloved family, Lord. Not my innocent brothers and sisters. Not the sweet Indian children. Not even the kind squaws, and a sannup or two. Not even the one sannup who held me in his arms through bittersweet nights and half made me forget I was an orphan, in a wretched family of orphans.

And my mistress. Let me speak for my dear mistress. She is goodness itself. She has promised me a dowry when I finish my service in her care. But whom shall I marry? And how much dowry? Think of mintmaster John Hull's daughter, lifted into one side of the mint-house scales, while servants heap the other side with pine-tree shillings until her weight is balanced! Negra settles me in one bowl of the stillroom scales and then heaps the other side with pumpkins. We laugh and laugh until tears stream down our cheeks.

Negra has heard gossip that Mr. Hull and others were selling Indians to her island for perpetual slaves. Mr. John Eliot, missionary to the Indians, appealed against the terror of such commerce. *The designs of Christ in these last days,* he has written, *are not to extirpate natives, but to gospelize them.* Mr. Hull once sent two Negro slaves from Boston to Madeira for sale, the returns to be made in red Madeira wine. To sell souls for money or wine seems to me a dangerous merchandising. I asked Mr. Mather about this. He replied: "Mr. Hull is scrupulous to enjoin his shipmaster to insist on the worship of God every day on the vessel, and to conduct his voyages to the sanctification of the Lord's Day and the suppression of profanities, that the Lord may delight to bless the ship's company and cargo." Mr. Mather himself boasts that as a young man he had the privilege of giving his father a fine Spanish Indian slave. Slavery is in the Bible.

To get back to horrorful Thomas Shepard. *Thy mind is a nest of all the foul opinions, heresies, that ever were vented by any man; thy heart is a foul sink of all atheism, sodomy, blasphemy, murder, whoredom, adultery, witchcraft, buggery; so that if thou hast any good thing in thee, it is but as a drop of rose-water in a bowl of poison; where fallen it is all corrupted.*

Dear God, is it true, is it true? Do I have all these black things in me? Even only a few? Even only adultery? Am I forgiven nothing? Spare me, dear God, such a grave burden! Bid me live hopeful and confident of my own innocent nature. Without faith, I cannot continue living. Dear Father in Heaven, are You so merciless a father?

My father in New Hampshire was a tender parent, as he was a tender shepherd to his flock. Often he likened us to gamboling lambs. And how many nights he sat up with the delivering ewe to cheer her in her difficult hours and ease her in the birthing. Dear Lord my Shepherd, care for me in Your husbandry! And if You must cut off my life, finish it swiftly and mercifully, even as my father dispatched the fattened ram in spring, yea, our favorite ram.

I wish I were a lamb in my father's arms, even the one to be slaughtered. Is the lamb's soul full of sin, too?

I think I must destroy these pages. Mr. Mather would not approve of my intimate addresses to God. I think I must throw these scribblings in the fire. Or hide them. Yes, I shall hide them. For I have an inclination to read them over tomorrow. I am comforted in my heart when I speak directly to God about my childhood. I miss my own childhood father even more than I miss God.

I wonder what kind of father Mr. Mather is to his children? Negra reminds me that he keeps his pockets full of baubles to give out to children. "Are you going to ask him, then, what kind of father he is? Are you, Mercy?" Dear silly Negra. I should not even be writing down the question. Certainly I cannot show these pages to him. What shall I show him, then? What can I write to satisfy him? I am tired of putting down the tricks of the Specters. I need tenderer thoughts to fill the long hours. Thoughts of hope, golden hope. Like the foamy wands of that willow out there in the yard. How goldenly they are swaying already in the February lengthening of daylight! How matted their skeins are soon to become in the looming March wind.

What if I should write only for myself? For myself alone, and not for Mr. Mather? What if I should hide these latest pages of my journal? Tell him I have consigned them to the fire? What if I should?

Mar. 4

Yesterday I boldly informed Mr. Mather that I am no longer keeping a journal. He was disappointed, all too clearly.

"I am fearful, Mercy, for your salvation," was all he said. But he looked deeply aggrieved.

I assured him that I shall relate aloud, as accurately in my selection of words as though I were writing them down, whatever might interest him. He has accepted my decision, a little testily. I have convinced him that my mind cannot be changed. Doubtless he thinks it's all the Devil's doing. Perhaps it is.

I must be alert about the journal itself, about where I hide it, and about being discovered writing in it. The Lord's Day, when everyone is at the meeting, is the best time for bringing the pages to light. My mistress suspects nothing. I have begged her to leave Negra with me on the Sabbath. My dear mistress consents, readily enough. I think she despairs of making a Christian of the girl. I can trust Negra. She comes from a gentler land. A warm, docile companion. Indeed I love the sweet girl.

And yet I miss the intense gatherings of folk praying and hymning for my recovery. Their enthusiasm excites me. I enjoy their furious agitation on my behalf. They must believe deeply in sin, else how could they exercise themselves so fervently against it? But they have lately grown somewhat cooler toward my sufferings. Are they losing interest in the haunted chamber? Are they beginning to question the gravity of my Bewitchment? They did once believe in it. What are they thinking of me now?

My mistress says that many persons have turned against the prosecutions in Salem last summer. Innocent citizens may have been hanged, on the evidence of hysterical children. Am I too a case of hysterical imaginings? Well, at least I am not a child, far from that. Negra says they mention my name in taverns and ordinaries, and with laughter rather than charity. What can they have heard? They mention Mr. Mather often, and without respect. Some townsmen are scoffing, railing or raving at Mr. Mather's special days of prayer. They blame him, among others, for the unjust executions in Salem. Folk are losing their orthodox convictions. The influence of Witchcraft is subsiding.

And lately my mistress, kind woman that she is, has begun to doubt the seriousness of my condition. I suspect my Bedevilment prolongs itself beyond her patience to bear with it. She asks if I cannot at least attend to my easy household tasks with more energy. She quotes Mr. Mather's medical treatise to the effect that *convenient EXERCISE does wonderfully conduce, not only to the preservation of health, but also to the recovery of it, by refreshing the faculties, by promoting the digestion, by quickening the glands in making their secretions, and many other ways.* Then she laughs, to show she is not serious as she tells about the Dutch and those of their criminals who refuse to work. The creatures are confined to a cellar, where water is let in upon them, *that they may be in a necessity either of pumping or of drowning.* Negra is trembling at the thought. It sounds a Devilish expedient to me.

Nowadays I am able to eat a little, every second or third day. I can work briefly, at simple chores, some mending, a bit of polishing. I shall force myself to eat more heartily. I believe by such means I shall please my mistress and finally defeat the Specters. Yet the truth is, my body is so weak, I cannot expect it to sustain my soul. My soul, my soul, I must consider my soul. And especially I must consider what I shall tell Mr. Mather about the progress of my spirit's fears and persecutions. For I must help him to maintain interest in me. I think this is now my chief task. I believe he is slipping gradually away from me. Is there a newer case of Bewitchment in the town? What if I should lose him entirely? What am I to do? He expects me to supply him with evidences, Devilish evidences. But the fact is, the Fiends are losing interest in me. The Fiends *and* Mr. Mather, Mr. Mather *and* the Fiends. Both at once. It is very strange. The Fiends are inclining to ignore me. But Mr. Mather *expects.*

Very well, I'll supply his expectations. I'll tell him, for instance, that the Imps are delighted to do many of my chores for me. I'll invent the instances. My mistress once blamed me for not carrying out the ashes, and the Devil cleared the hearth for me afterwards. Negra will not give me away. I'll tell him that the Specters have torn a page of the Bible, one of Mr. Mather's own, which he left for me. Did he think they would not dare damage a Bible because it was his? But I think I have already invented some such outrage. He must not grow suspicious. He might question past complaints.

Well then, let me be very sly, very interesting. I'll tell him how I am often visited by Unknown Shapes and forced away with them, to unknown places where I witness meetings, feastings, dancings. At such times they knock me with a blow on the back, whereupon I am ever as if bound with chains, uncapable of stirring out of the place, till they release me. I'll tell him of promises to give me splendid garments if I but sign their book. They threaten me often with flames. Negra will confirm that the room has smelled of brimstone. The agonies of roasting at the stake are not more exquisite than the scalds those Hell-hounds give me, sometimes for nearly a quarter of an hour at a time. I'll employ wild expressive gestures. I'll seize the minister's hand in my ardor, and secretly slip the gold ring off his finger. Later I'll ask him if he does not miss it. Then I'll tell him where to find it. And I'll warn him not to put it on again, or the Specters will lop off his finger.

Negra suggests I concoct a story of a great black cat jumping over her, Fiendishly, in order to tear at my body. If Mr. Mather should question the truth of my claims, I'll threaten to pull open my gown and show him Devil-inspired blisters on my breast. I'll moan and call out for salad oil to comfort the wounds. I'll tell him of a thousand excruciating pains all over my body, which are, however, cured immediately, that they may be at once repeated. I'll shriek so close to his ear he'll be startled into leaving the room. But then I'll draw him back by carrying on highly charged conversations with the Devil at the top of my lungs.

"Why do you rail and slander," I'll shout, "against

a certain Godly minister? He is praying to Heaven that I be saved. Don't you dare try to torment him! He is beyond the reach of your Infernal stabs and scourings. He is a man above reproach, most resembling an Angel, and not a fallen one like your Instigator! You talk of carrying me to Heaven! Ho! ho! What Heaven would that be? Whither did you carry the Witch Martha Carrier, lately hanged at Salem? Answer me that! You say you keep your servants alive, beyond the power of the Lord in Heaven! Ha! Then why did you let the halter choke your minions last summer in Salem?"

I'll pause to let Mr. Mather see me beating frantically at the Fiends. Then I'll struggle to draw my breath, and go on.

"I admit you were once a resident of Heaven, yes. But God for your pride hurled you thence. He that has the Devil for his leader must be content with Hell for his lodging! Hell! You lying Wretch, I have caught you in a hundred falsehoods! The other day you told me there was no Hell; and now you tell me that a sinner may come out of Hell! Well then, let Sarah Good come out of Hell! She it was who first put me under your malign influence. If all the wood in the world were laid in one fire, it would not be so awful as Hell!"

And so on and so on.

Perhaps Mr. Mather will come with a chorus of faithful neighbors when next he visits me. I have begged him to bring them once again. Their voices drown out the blasphemies of the Fiend. They are such a spirited company. I like to be surrounded by them, by the light of their ardent countenances. It is like basking in the noon sun. I hope they have not lost patience with me. What is it they wish from me?

Am I no longer sufficiently Bedevilled to interest them? Must I stir up the Fiend, to please them? Do they suspect that I am now feigning? That in fact I have quite recovered from Fiendish influences? Would they like to believe, like Mr. Mather himself, that I triumphed over the Specters on the eve of the New Year, once and for all?

Alas, I did not finally triumph then. I was simply weary of being cooped up like a creature in a cage. I craved, more than salvation, fresh air, fresh clothes, fresh surroundings. It served my despondent purpose to seem indeed recovered. Mr. Mather, with his long acquaintance among sinners and their symptoms, should have known better. One does not break off with one's history as the day breaks off with night. The sun itself creates new shadows. Some shadows will haunt me all my days.

Are folk avoiding my haunted chamber? Alas, their souls no longer agitate for my soul. Let Mr. Mather keep his faith in me.

Something cheerful, how sorely I need something cheerful to pass the hours until the minister's next visit. My mistress encourages me to read books from her library. I choose pious reading when there is anybody about. Mr. Mather has reminded me more than once: "There are, they say, 200,000 books in the library which Ptolemy erected at Alexandria; but it was the addition of the Scriptures which made it a truly LEARNED library."

On the Lord's Day, when I am alone or with no one but Negra, I like to bring out the volume by Thomas Morton and copy some of the pages. He did so love this land, its beauty and fruitfulness. I like to read aloud to Negra. We are both deeply enchanted, in a blissful way, by his descriptions.

*Goodly groves of trees, dainty fine round rising
hillocks, delicate fair large plains, sweet crystal
fountains, and clear running streams, that twine in
fine meanders through the meads, making so sweet a
murmuring noise to hear, as would even lull the
senses with delight asleep, so pleasantly do they glide
upon the pebble stones, jetting most jocundly where
they do meet. . . .*

Oh I think he is describing Heaven itself, such a
Paradise it sounds! Bliss-land! And Negra says it is
an exact description of the land she remembers from
her childhood. I must copy more of these ravishing
words.

*Fowls in abundance, fish in multitude, and discovered
besides, millions of turtle-doves on the green boughs,
which sat pecking of the full ripe pleasant grapes that
were supported by the lusty trees, whose fruitful load
did cause the arms to bend . . .*

What Divine praise! What eloquence! How I
should love to have known the writer of such tribute
to our teeming land! Pointing to the book on the
shelf, *The New English Canaan*, I once asked my mistress about the author. "He was called Lord of Mis-
rule, for his pagan practices. It is said he set up a
maypole with drinking and dancing about it for
many days together."

"What is the evil of the maypole?"

"Such revelry, dear Mercy, is not our Christian
practice. Moreover, Thomas Morton and his fellows
at Merry Mount invited Indian women for their con-
sorts, and frolicked and feasted like so many beastly
Bacchanalians. A dangerous fellow. Firearms and

firewater were what the savages most coveted, and what was forbidden by our English. Only Thomas Morton defied the Christian practice. Mr. Mather would hardly wish you to read his book."

But Thomas Morton describes those revels and merriment as an old English custom. Last May a maypole in Charlestown was cut down by official order, and then a bigger one was set up in defiance, with a garland around it and a pair of buckhorns nailed to the top. They say it was a fair sea-mark.

What can be so sinful about celebrating the return of spring? Heaven knows I cannot bear waiting for it to arrive on these shores and freshen this jaded city like a great salt wave on an arid beach. The groundhog peered out hesitantly and then plunged back into his hole a month ago. Within the coming fortnight he should emerge to stay and feed and fatten. Shall I emerge with him? Shall I at last rouse from this winter stupor and create my life anew? Negra says she has heard that the women of Europe roll naked in the dew before sunrise on May Day morning, and are assured of good fortune throughout the year. Let us try the ritual together! Swear that you will, Negra! And we shall look down a well reflected in a mirror and see, each of us, the face of her future husband. I know what face I shall hope to see. And what sweet voice I shall hear rising from the bottom of the well. And not a hymn tune, for that matter!

O Negra, let us dance, dance, dance around a maypole till our beautiful dresses fall to the ground! If we Boston Christians are not allowed to celebrate Christmas and the winter solstice with music and revelry, let us at least rejoice in the merrymaking fullness of spring!

Look, here in *The New English Canaan* is a truly

Godly passage. The saintly Mr. Mather himself could not object to it.

Children and the fruit of the womb are said in holy writ to be an inheritance that cometh of the Lord. Happy is that land and blessed too that is apt and fit for increase of children.

Was my fruit, the secret fruit of my womb, its darkened skin and river-gray eyes, an inheritance coming from the Lord? Who can answer my sore questioning? Oh might I be cured by the waters of the fountain of Merry Mount!

Nectar is a thing assigned
By the Deity's own mind
To cure the heart oppressed with grief.

Everyone knows that Thomas Morton was driven out of our land for his infamous consorting with the Indians. But I remember the tribesmen spoke well of him. And he himself has written in his book that he was envied for the prosperity of his beaver trade and therefore plotted against. Is it surprising he found the New England Indians more full of humanity than the Christians? Until the moment of the massacre my father traded peaceably and profitably with the natives.

Much later this Lord's day evening, Mr. Mather comes by with a small chorus of young men, Joseph Marshall among them. I was chiefly concerned lest I appear too calm, too reasonable to require their ministrations. I greeted the good folk, all except the particular young man, most effusively. Something prevented me from acknowledging his presence. Heaven knows I could not fail to notice him. In my need to keep the company with me as long as possible, I found myself inventing a series of *plagues,* in which my tortures were turned into frolics, and I became as extravagant as a wildcat. I behaved so disordered, I called the visitors by wrong and fanciful names: *Temptation Moody, Fitfulness Smith, Wrath-o'-God Wiggins.* Of course I knew who they were.

I had an impulse to show off the excellence of my spelling, a sudden strange compulsion. I lettered out a whole series of difficult words to impress the listeners: *lithobolia,* as in stone-throwing; *coscinomancy,* as in sieve-divination; *quadragesima,* as in forty days of Lent; *crepitate,* as of snakes rattling; *enchiridon,* a manual of Demons; *Euroclydon,* that tempestuous wind which arises in ACTS 27:14; *emunctories,* the body's organs which excrete; *amplexus,* sexual embrace of the toad.

I felt an irresistible desire to be insolent, abusive, though never downright profane. I took liberties such as pulling Mr. Mather's wig. In my impertinence I quoted MATTHEW 5:36– *Neither shalt thou swear by thy head, because thou canst not make one hair white or black.* "Ho, ho!" I went on. "You call it but an innocent fashion? I suppose you would fain wear it for your health? I had not expected to hear a predication of periwigs in a Boston pulpit by Mr. Mather!"

I became wildly excited and, as I thought, witty. I hectored the poor minister with blows of my fists and kicks of my feet, though they would always recoil when they were within an inch or two of him, as if rebounding against a wall. I reeled and spewed, as though in drunken confusion. I marched right up to Joseph Marshall and embraced him.

"Where were you conceived?" I cried. "In a field

of cornflowers? That's how blue your eyes are!"

I seized his hands and whirled him round and round, then flung him away. By myself I danced and pranced around the room, overturning the candles and nearly setting the house on fire.

I threw myself at Mr. Mather's feet and begged him to help me overcome the Fiends.

"*Ephialtes!*" I cried. "The Devil is hounding me into dread *Ephialtes!* You yourself have written that such nightmares lead to apoplexy, epilepsy, mania! Pray for me, Mr. Mather! Fast and pray for me against the Wizards!"

He threw his arms about me, so hard I gasped for breath.

"Tell 'em," he shouted, himself like one possessed, "that the Lord Jesus Christ has broken the Old Serpent's head!" He seemed wondrously irradiated. At that moment I knew for a shining certitude that nothing is too hard for God.

Now I am writing by the light of a full midnight moon. Everyone is asleep, even Negra lying beside me. It is so still, I can almost hear the beans sprouting in their dish on the windowsill. How bravely they crack their shell and stretch their body into the strange air. *Air! Air!*

An owl is hooting into the silence. I hope our new kitten is safe indoors. I hope the young owlets are safe in their shelter. I have seen an owl pecked to death on its nest. Rather than desert its young, it remained at the mercy of a mob of crows who attacked with raucous cries. My sister and I, crossing to the barn at daybreak, saved the little ones from the parent's fate. Those hateful shrieks of marauding crows! They were scarcely less harsh than the howlings of wolves. Or of massacre-bent Indians.

Yet it has been told that during King Philip's war, not so long ago, Indian women were found lying naked on the ground, their heads cut off and stuck on poles. Can Englishmen have committed such savagery? What is to be believed? It is a certainty that King Philip himself was beheaded and quartered; and his widow and children sold into West Indian slavery.

If God is a great forgiver, can I not be a small one? The Tawnies themselves were good forgivers. They never, not once on the march, reminded me that I had picked up a poker from the hearth of our already surrounded house, and beaten like a madwoman at every enemy within my reach, until one sannup gently—now I remember how gently—disarmed me. Others spoke to me in quiet voices, as kindly as a father. In some sage fashion of their own, they calmed me. I should not forget that gentleness is often their prevailing mood.

And cheerful competence. The midwives, for instance, so expert, so heartening. The squaws are strong in their procreation, and very lusty following delivery. And while they are with child, and as great as can be, they do not avoid heavy tasks. I have seen them in that condition with burdens on their backs enough to load a horse, yet they do not complain, nor do they miscarry. Toward my own condition they always showed a particular tenderness. Though they expected me to keep up with the pace of the march at all times, never once did they overburden me. And when my labor came upon me many weeks before expected, they cared for me as their own dearest daughter. Strangely, there are times when I recall my captivity as no more grievous than the poignance of some pleasure, such a pleasure as picking the terse blackberry, that *jeweled ripener,* whose bramble rasps the wrist.

I was proud to discover that it took me no longer than the lustiest squaw to be delivered of babe and afterbirth, to stand on my feet, and join the moving band. I think I was most like those Hebrew women in the Egyptian captivity, whom God made so lively they commonly delivered themselves before a midwife could arrive to help them.

The squaws made a bath of walnut leaves and husks to stain the infant's skin, which was fairish. They dipped and washed until it was tawny. His hair was black as his father's. His eyes were gray as a clear river. A cradle was made for the child, a board forked on both ends, whereon the child was fast bound, and wrapped in furs. He was placed in a proper position, his knees thrust up towards his belly. This method is found to develop the race into well-proportioned men and women. Thus they guard against crooked backs or wry legs. They called him *nan weeteo,* which is a bastard. His eyes were much admired by all the tribe because they were a novelty among that nation. But the child did not thrive long. Perhaps it is dangerous to mix the races.

The moon has set. Soon it will be dawn.

> *How glorious are the morning stars!*
> *How doth their glory shine!*

The kitten is indoors, praise be! It has crept to my bed, mewing forlornly. I shall take it in with me and comfort it. I wish I were nursing a blue-eyed baby.

Mar. 11

What a week it has been! The happiest week of my life since before the massacre! I have truly come to my senses, and everyone must see the change in me. It began on Monday morning, when my mistress said, "You are well enough, Mercy, to do an errand for me. Negra will accompany you. Go to one of the booksellers at the Town House."

It is not surprising, is it, that of all the twenty booksellers in Boston, all of them clustered at the Town House, I chose to go to the one where Joseph Marshall is employed? How my heart was beating as I walked, no, *ran,* past the twenty-one pillars supporting the overhanging storeys of the building, till I reached the premises I was seeking! The shop had only one of the two books my mistress had requested, but that did not matter. Joseph Marshall promised to deliver the other to our dwelling later in the week. I browsed intently among the shelves, and took my time about leaving. I am right about his eyes. He came to the door with me when I finally could not pretend to a reason for staying longer. They are indeed the color of cornflowers.

"Cornflowers," I murmured to myself.

"What about cornflowers?" I had not thought he heard me.

"Your eyes, the very color! But your voice is an orchis. Do you know the orchis?"

"The plant we call dogstones? With the roundish tuberoids? I once took notice of a wanton woman's compounding the solid roots with wine for an amorous cup, which wrought the desired effect."

"Oh, perhaps not the same."

"You must point it out to me some day. And I shall show you the woadwaxen, your hair's color."

"Oh, you mean Witches' Blood."

"Of course. Clear, teasing yellow. You must have been conceived on Gallows Hill!"

"No, indeed. Near Salmon Falls."

"Ah, that accounts for the color and behavior of your slippery tongue! Do you know what the Roman naturalist writes about the salmon?"

"How should I know *that*?"

"Because it concerns you, you before all others. *The river salmon surpasseth all the fishes of the sea.*"

The early spring light was dazzling. The pebbled paving of cobblestones brought up from the beaches and laid down close-fitting looked freshly washed, and glinted like a pathway of semi-precious gems. Merchants, shipmasters and strangers moved among the sheltered passages along the Town House pillars. I seized Negra's hand and raced up and down highways, cartways and wheelbarrow ways, lanes and alleys, like a creature possessed. Possessed, but not Satanically. No, possessed with the joy of being in the midst of my life. My dark years were behind me, behind me my Demons and my deaths. "God is a great forgiver!" I cried to Negra as we hurtled home by many detours. I laughed and blew a kiss at the fat constable who tried to chase us, shaking his long black staff.

"Slow down!" he cried, but we could not, in spite of the heavy traffic of carts, horses, wagons and carriages that threatened from one moment to the next to impede us. We darted in and out of obstacles, and interrupted the boys' games of wickets. Somebody's cow was wandering at large in front of Salutation Tavern, in the way of all procedure, human, equine, and wheeled. Rounding a corner, we bumped into Judge Sewall hunting for the lost creature. We shouted out merry directions to him.

He thanked us heartily. "How healthy you look, Mercy!" he cried. "I am glad to see you so wholesomely restored." We waved good-bye and ran on. Judge Sewall has taken a keen interest in my condition of Bewitchment, and indeed in my entire welfare here in Boston ever since I was ransomed over two years ago. But I remember him from several years before that, when he came to Salmon Falls during the short masting season, to watch a great tree being brought down and drawn out of the swamp by three dozen oxen.

"I am glad for the sake of your masting team that this tree does not bear the *broad arrow* sign of the Royal Navy," said Judge Sewall to my father. "I rejoice with you that the King's surveyor overlooked this monumental specimen. And I am gratified to see our colonists reaping at least a portion of their rewards for laboring in this splendid timber land."

Remembering those great giants of our forest, even taller trees than Judge Sewall's, I pulled Negra toward the Bay. I longed to see close above me the soaring columns, and to recall the excitement of watching the mast-cutters at their work. Here we stood, now on one wharf, now on another, built out along piles, amid many fair shops made of brick, stone, and lime, and handsomely contrived. A whole navy of idle masts rose above us, while I described to Negra the careful preparations of our masting teams.

"My father let me watch the spectacle at a safe distance. A path along level ground had to be cleared from the base in the direction in which the tree would fall. Larger branches of the mast tree had to be cut away. Smaller branches were left to gentle the force of the fall. The men probed for hidden obstacles under the snow: covered logs, stumps, rocks. Then a deep blanket of more snow and leaves was laid along the path. And finally the hewing! Oh the thrill as the woodsmen's blows halted and the first splintering sounds were followed by huge thundering roars of a giant crashing to earth! Look, Negra, look at those giants soaring above us! Some day I should like to sail away at the tip of such a mast! I can feel myself hovering light as a leaf, between Heaven and Earth!"

Negra fairly had to drag me home, so reluctant I was to leave the wharf.

"What kept you so long?" cries my mistress at the door. But she does not pause for an answer. "Oh my dear Mercy, your cheeks are red as rose-fire! I do believe you are becoming yourself again!"

After finishing, with unaccustomed zest, my tasks for the day, I borrowed the new book from my mistress, who had, indeed, ordered it because of the interest my history had aroused. Mrs. Rowlandson's captivity, in 1675, was much shorter than mine, but filled with quite as much sorrow. There was hunger and there was feasting, as on our march. And incidents of cruelty and of kindness, both. The author takes special account of behavior between men and women: Red men and White women. In the end, she parted on friendly terms with her captors, some asking her to send them bread, others tobacco, a sannup shaking her by the hand, giving her a hood and scarf to ride in. One Indian even offered, early in her captivity, to run away to her home, with his squaw as well. But she declined. She declares: *I have been in the midst of those roaring lions and savage bears, by night and day, alone and in company; sleeping all sorts together, and yet not one of them ever offered the least abuse of unchastity to me, in word or action. Though some English are ready to say I speak it for my own credit.*

I think I must be one of 'em, one of those English, for I am ready to say she does indeed write as in self-praise. Moreover, she was not a country girl of fifteen years.

Mrs. Rowlandson lost a daughter, as I a son. All night she lay with her dead babe. Well I know she suffered the deepest of all losses. Is it not the more surprising that she could write so heartlessly of the death of her squaw's papoose? *And there was one benefit in it, that there was more room.*

More room! I have never heard a Tawny utter so pitiless a sentiment. The cruel record continues: *I went to a wigwam, and they bid me come in, and gave me a skin to lie upon, and a mess of venison and groundnuts. On the morrow they buried the papoose; and afterward, both morning and evening, there came a company to mourn and howl with her. Though I confess I could not much condole with them.* Shame on Mrs. Rowlandson! She reveals herself harsher than her very captors. As for myself, I remember only tender condolences. Is it necessary to bear a half-Indian babe before one can judge the tribesmen fairly?

Nor can I believe Mrs. Rowlandson's account of a poor woman very big with child, having but one week further to reckon. According to this report, the woman would often be asking the Indians to let her go home. This they were unwilling to do, and grew vexed with her importunities. *They gathered a great company together about her, and stripped her naked and set her in the midst of them; and when they had sung and danced about her (in their Hellish manner) as long as they pleased, they knocked her on the head, repeatedly. When they had done that, they made a fire and put her in it, and told the other children that were with her, that if they attempted to go home they would serve them in like manner.* A Fiendish behavior, but I do not believe it. To be sure, unchastity would be a very small sin, too negligible to be engaged in, for such monsters as Mrs. Rowlandson has invented. Dreary woman, she fairly *wallows* in her persecutions.

Mr. Mather has reminded me that the devout should offer a given hour every Monday to pray for persecuted churches abroad. I murmur a few lines from the Psalms, but my heart is not in it.

I slept miserably all night, with Demonic echoes rattling through my dreams, and occasional cornflowers sprouting like horns from a Fiend's goatish head. Negra says I cried out blasphemies from time to time. She hushed and comforted me. She knows it is now expedient, nay, essential, that I overcome all traces of Bewitchment without delay.

Tuesday was rainy and warmish, not a refreshing downpour, just a drizzle-drozzle. I kept indoors, and went about my duties sluggishly. The forsythia branches, brought indoors last week, are already in golden bloom. Outside my window an alder is loosening its purple catkin clusters into ruddy lengths.

The tangled willow yarns look as though the kitten has got into them. I have been keeping close account of the six-foot branch of dogwood knocked down some weeks ago by a heavy storm. It stands in a vase of water at the east window. I have watched the little dead-brown bracts split into twin shingles overlapping. I have seen the inner spring-green cheeks pushed apart by a dozen sudden tongues. Overnight the stone life turned chalice, a four-scaled cup. Now here I sit attending, a rapt witness to this transient miracle of nature. I am dizzy with watching. I feel about to slip out of this world.

"Look at it!" I cry to Negra. "Look at the pearly moth-wings, their need to leave the branch, the stem they once belonged to! To forget the garden they grew in, and the town where grew the garden! See *me*, my moth-wings! *Me!* I am leaving, Negra! I have a fury to be myself! I am the secret in the bud, the hidden rage to live my life, my very own life! Hold me tight, Negra! Help me hold on to my life!"

And that sweet small life which like a foamy dogwood blossom endured so briefly—might I have cherished it, protected it, suckled it with deeper devotion? Am I to blame, that it was extinguished? That I lost my milk, its sustenance? Did those Indian squaws have the required wisdom of nourishments and cures which are known to our Boston English? I have read, over and over again, what Mr. Mather has written about methods of increasing milk. *The water wherein fresh fish has been boiled will fetch back the nurse's milk, and will so supply her breasts that they shall be better to the infant than the richest cluster of the vine. The infant may suckle and be satisfied.*

My mistress is accustomed to quote Mr. Mather's medical treatises on every suitable occasion, always with utmost faith and respect. His reputation regarding medicaments is considerable. Indeed, it is said that there was a time in his youth when his stammer proved so alarming, his father became determined on a career as physician for him, rather than as minister. I do not always take comfort in Mr. Mather's medical advice, however learned. *Take powder of earthworms,* for instance, *to insure a rich milk supply.* With a wry humor he counsels the reader of this chapter not to expect that she'll become like the French nurse *who not only suckled at once a couple of boys, but also from her milk supplied an apothecary with butter, which he found the noblest remedy in the world for a consumption.* Such jesting exaggeration offends me. Where is the dignity of his office? Where is compassion for the deprived and grieving mother?

When I regained consciousness I was lying on the floor, in Negra's arms. She was bathing my face with a cool damp cloth, and singing a lullaby from her native island. "Was the Devil bothering you again?" she asked me. I shook my head, no. When I could speak, I told her this was no Devil but rather a glorious Angel who swept me away in a faint. I felt confused, but strangely comforted. I was glad my mistress had gone to visit a sick neighbor. I would not have wanted her to see me in my helplessness. Such behavior is no longer acceptable. I want her to believe that I am quite well again.

I was pleased that she had not yet returned by the time Joseph Marshall lifted the brass knocker on the front door, at the same moment singing out a lively tune. Oh, that throbbing voice! It nearly caused me to faint again. I asked him to come in, and to wait, quite properly, for my mistress's return. We sat silent for a few awkward minutes. Then we both started up suddenly with talk of the weather, the early warmth and signs of spring, the nearness of the vernal equinox. I went silent again. But Joseph Marshall went on sturdily, describing a big launching of a vessel one day last week, in the sight of hordes of townsfolk. I have heard Mr. Mather criticize the foolish profane custom of a mock-baptism, but of course I made no solemn comment. Earlier in the week a porpoise was pursued and taken within the inward wharfs. How eloquently Joseph Marshall tells the story! Even his speaking voice is full of manly music.

I was gathering my courage to beg him for a song, a tune just for Negra and me, some popular ballad, not a psalm, when my mistress returned. She thanked him for the religious treatise he had brought, and asked him if his shop had a copy of the book *Pilgrim's Progress*. She said she was planning to give me a copy of my own. I think I could do without the Bunyan volume, but I thanked her all the same. Of course I rejoiced at the prospect of seeing Joseph Marshall so soon again.

My mistress told me to watch the Westfield pork being roasted for our dinner. Just about noon our kitchen chimney fell on fire, and blazed out sorely at the top, appearing to be very foul. The fire fell directly on shingles so that they began to burn in several places. No great harm was done, and we sat merrily to dinner on the pork snatched from the blaze.

Wednesday dragged tediously. With the exceedingly mild spell of weather, we made an early start in our spring cleaning. The house began to shine fragrantly with the glow and aroma of beeswax polish. I had a terrible fright when the sweep sent down a hen through the chimney from the roof where he was working. He was only cleaning the passage, he said, but I thought a Demon in the form of a fowl had spun down to assail me. It took all the self-command in my possession to tell myself: "No, Mercy Short, no! You are no longer Bedevilled! Your life is in your own hands. And God's, of course. And Mr. Mather's. And maybe, in some blessed future, Joseph Marshall's." And I prayed more fervently than ever in my whole life. I sang a vigorous hymn while I churned the butter. Over and over I sang it, till my mistress commented on my choice of text. But I laughed, still churning, and sang one more time:

> Let him with kisses of his mouth
> Be pleased me to kiss.

I took for cheerful sign the black-spotted beetle, crimson as dawning hope, crawling up a window out of its winter sleep. Spring me, dear Light, from my winter cranny!

Thursday, market day, I was sent to fetch the Bunyan book, as well as fresh produce for our supper. The town sparkled, bright and bustling. A brilliant shaft of sun was caught for a moment on the coils of the Green Dragon sign hanging on an iron crane that projected from the tavern wall. But while I stared the tail curled tighter, and the fearful tongue thrust itself toward me. I pulled myself away, and ran on till I found a cluster of boys playing at marbles. I knelt and tried to join them, but they elbowed me away.

I moved on, breathing in the deep, mysterious smell of lumber and cattle and hay brought from New Hampshire through the port, and now being transported to the market center near the Town House. Over Boston Neck, from neighboring towns, had crawled a parade of oxcarts bearing firewood, charcoal, salt fish, furs, country produce, and all kinds of wooden articles made in the long dark winter. Country folk had come with freshly slaughtered chickens and lambs. Large buckets of hens' eggs shone like polished nuggets in the sun. Apples and squashes and onions from last autumn's harvest were stacked neatly and temptingly. I hurried past a public whipping, without even inquiring the nature of the offense. It was a day for celebration, not for punishment.

Forgetful of my errands, I sauntered after a small herd of cows being driven to the burying ground and the Common for grazing. At one point, some oxen penned in a yard grew agitated over the passing cows, and pounded the grass and damp ground under their feet into dozens of muddy footprints. I had to laugh at their poor unsatisfied arousal. I found a small dry rock on the Common, and sat down to rest.

In front of me soared the damaged and patched bole of a sycamore. I looked more carefully and saw the cream-gold beginnings of new bark. Always new beginnings, I breathed. Even though the old seed-balls still hung on the branches. How calm, how content I felt in these surroundings. If only I could keep forever this peace of heart! I hummed and wove a poem into place.

> That's how I'd like to sing,
> soft as a plush burr,
> a tarnished tawny ball,
> not jarring the spell of March,
> just minding the promising air,
> humming the whole good news
> of April to come.

Let April come in without knocking! For the year is a turning stile. Here I am seated, one more spring again, under this great elm bristling with buds. See how the elm comes curving into the year's spring-tide, one circuit more, one more loosening of bud-scales into a coppery mist. Was it on this tree, from its very boughs, that Quakers were hanged? "The zeal of this country," says Mr. Mather, "formerly had in it more fire than should have been; especially when the deranged Quakers were sent unto the gallows, that should have been kept rather in a bedlam."

And the Witch Ann Hibbins, and poor mad Mrs. Dorothy Talbye who murdered her daughter, Difficult, of the prophetic name? How I rejoice in my name: *Mercy!* Let there be a downpouring of Heaven's mercy upon me, to match my name! Let there be no more Bedevilments, no more Witches and no more hangings, I murmured, spreading my arms wide to the still leafless air. I stayed and watched the movements and pauses of the whole world stretched out before me. Cows grazing, children playing, man and maid walking hand in hand or stopping to converse intimately face to face, groups of volunteer militia engaged in their training. My little world, my loved little world.

A long time passed before I remembered that I had started out on errands for my mistress. I stood up in haste and crossed to where the Province House rose, three-storeyed and proud, set disdainfully back from the High Street. A fine new young fuzz of lawn flanked the paved walk to the great red stone entrance steps. The two statuesque oaks seemed to converse loftily with each other across the pavement, like splendid superior beings. I looked up beyond the columned portico, beyond the balcony on its roof, to the cupola, upon which stood the Indian archer weathervane. Proud in the midafternoon light, his glass eyes gleaming mysteriously, he forever drew his bow. I felt a moment's shudder, turned abruptly, and found myself facing an Indian whose features I thought I recognized. A piece of his ear was cut off, doubtless for burglary. But he moved on without a sign of recognition.

A wind had come up, unexpectedly sharp. I ran home as though the Indian—the one on the cupola, the one on the street, I can't say which—were chasing me. Only upon reaching our threshold did I remember the neglected errands. My mistress opened the door for me. I started to apologize, but she stopped me, her hand on my mouth.

"Joseph Marshall has been here, my darling Mercy, and he has asked permission to court you. I have given my consent. Now all that is needed is *yours!*"

Mine? *Mine!*

I threw myself at her with a wild embrace that nearly tumbled both of us onto the pebbles of the path. My heart heaved up, sank down, heaved up again, enormously, like those long slender pines hefted from crest to trough to crest in a wind-lashed pond on the Piscataqua, awaiting the mast fleet from England. My mistress drew me indoors, where Negra, all benign smiles, waited in a sunlit corner. The red sun from horizon level illuminated her face like an exotic bloom. Her teeth gleamed like precious royal gems. "Oh Negra," I cried, hugging her harder than I intended, making her gasp, "your teeth are so beautiful! Don't ever let any Devilish sin spoil them!" She promised faithfully.

Pilgrim's Progress, left by Joseph Marshall, lay on a bench by the hearth. I picked it up roughly, having a sudden desire to hurl it into the flames. Just in time, however, a surprising change of heart came into me. I put the book down gently as rare glass. I shall try to read it calmly, without undue credence, as I might skim a fairy tale. For I am a rash girl no longer. I am a woman facing the blessed prospect of marriage.

> *When in this knot I planted was, my stock*
> *Soon knotted, and a manly flower out brake.*

When I am planted in this knot of wedlock, shall a manly flower, another sweet manly flower outbreak?

There is now little time for journal-keeping. I have declared myself cured of Bewitchment, and Mr. Mather is free to devote himself to another young woman lately fallen victim to malign influences. Though I am sorry for Margaret Rule, I think I am glad for Mr. Mather, for the exercise of his vocation. He rejoices in my deliverance. "The Devil got just nothing, but God got praises, Christ got subjects, the Holy Spirit got temples, the church got addition, and the souls of men got everlasting benefits."

All this from my rescue out of Bedevilment?

"Never forget, Mercy, the Millennium is at hand, hardly four years hence, precisely in 1697!"

I asked how he could be certain.

"I have computed the Second Coming by adding 180 years to the date of Luther's Reformation!" Mr. Mather's face was illumined with bliss.

I shall attend the meeting next Sunday, and tell all who are willing to listen that I am the betrothed of Joseph Marshall. I think I shall have the temerity to ask Mr. Mather for a special hymn in our honor: Anne Bradstreet's joyous text.

> *As spring the winter doth succeed,*
> *And leaves the naked trees do dress,*
> *The earth all black is clothed in green—*

And blue is the color of my true love's eyes!

Next year, by the time of the summer solstice, I shall have finished my service in this house. The *summer standing still!* My heart stands still at the very thinking of it! Doubtless my soul, as well. Oh if only I might go to my wedding upon a white horse, and wearing a gown of scarlet satin with a purple velvet shoulder cloak over it! And ribbons, ribbons, ribbons in the wreath on my hair. A double rainbow of ribbons! So much bleakness of my life must be amended finally! A marriage such as has never been witnessed in the Puritan town of Boston!

Now to the prospect at hand: the third week of March, the solemn third anniversary of the destruction of my beloved Salmon Falls, and the deaths that attended it. Let this observance be my final mourning. From this moment forth let me no longer dwell on morbid memories. The scars of past sorrows shall be no more memorable than the small crescents the ash tree is wearing under its buds, insignia of past stems and seasons. Farewell to past seasons! Welcome to my new life!

Welcome to the imminent arrival of the vernal equinox! My hours and days of light henceforth grow longer. My eleven months of salamander darkness are ended. I shall stay in the Light. I am a young woman much blest, with greater blessings yet to come. Mr.

Mather speaks of me as a *brand pluck'd out of the burning.* I pray God he has not singed his fingers.

> *My winter's spent, my storms are gone,*
> *And former clouds seem now all fled.*

Next year, come summer, I shall sign myself, in truth and devotion,

Mercy Short Marshall

Postscript

*She was finally and forever delivered from the hands
of evil Angels; and I had afterwards the Satisfaction
of seeing not only her so brought home unto the Lord,
that she was admitted unto our Church, but also
many other, even some scores, of young People,
awakened by the Picture of Hell, exhibited in her
Sufferings, to flee from the Wrath to come.*

Cotton Mather, DIARY, 1693

*Mercy Marshall, whom I had formerly, with many
cries to Heaven, rescued from the Hand of evil
Angels, being found guilty of adultery, had the
highest Censure of Excommunication this day passed
upon her.*

Cotton Mather, DIARY, 1698